11TH MAY 1984

Author from a Savage People

Born in Milwaukee, Wisconsin, Bette Pesetsky has been awarded a grant from the National Endowment for the Arts. Married to a Professor of Medicine at the Albert Einstein School of Medicine, she has one son. *Stories up to a Point* was her first collection of short stories.

D1143777

Bette Pesetsky

Author from a Savage People

Pavanne
published by Pan Books

First published in Great Britain 1983 by The Bodley Head Ltd
This Pavanne edition published 1984 by Pan Books Ltd,
Cavaye Place, London SW10 9PG
© Bette Pesetsky 1983
ISBN 0 330 28250 6
Photoset by Parker Typesetting Service
Printed and bound in Great Britain by
Collins, Glasgow

'You're savages,' the politician said.

'Women are savages. I've always known that.

Civilization has never reached women.'

Political Sayings – Anonymous

One

"Sit," said the policeman. We sat. The long bench had no back. I leaned against the wall, resting my head, my good shoulder, and my good arm. Now I had a good shoulder and a good arm because I also had bad ones.

The old woman who sat next to me looked like a rented relative. She sat sunk down on the slick wood, collapsed like a dented cushion—the feathers of her body definitely needing a plumping up. When her upholstery started stretching towards me, I pulled back. But did I look like such a good piece of furniture myself?

I looked like nothing—old slacks with a well-polished seat, fuzz-ball sweater. I didn't even have a comb. I looked like worse than nothing—and weren't appearances everything? So how had I arrived at this thrift-shop condition?

It was a newspaper. A newspaper and the actions of a vengeful God.

"It's quiet," the old woman said to me. "But what can you expect on a Wednesday? Not close to a holiday, either. You should see it then."

"Right," I said. I was against the wall feeling the cold plaster. Further retreat was impossible.

"An ER is never what you expect," the old woman said.

"A what?"

"Oh ho," she said, "a first-timer. ER is what we call the emergency room. Not what you'd expect, it it? No Dr. Gillespie on wheels. Look, for instance, at the walls. Coat of paint wouldn't hurt. See that door? Know what's behind it? Mops and buckets. Not doctors—mops and buckets."

"ER," I said.

The old woman sighed and sank lower, belly on lap, breasts on belly. "My friend is coming out from Brooklyn to pick me up. I told him don't take the subway. Get the Pontiac from the garage. If you don't live far, we could drop you."

"Thank you," I said, "but someone is coming. A friend."

We both turned to watch the policeman with the new arrivals. "Sit," the policeman said. The two men sat on the other end of the bench. Each man wore a turban of white gauze.

The old woman pressed closer. Were they dangerous? We didn't know. We heard a noise, a yelling. We turned as a man ran down the hall towards us. He was chasing a small boy, a boy about four years old. The boy wore a grey sweater. The man carried a stick in his hand, something supple, something like a switch. "I'll get you," the man cried. The boy pushed at a swinging door and vanished behind it, the man followed. We turned to the policeman.

"A weapon," I said.

"A twig," the policeman said.

I looked at the old woman. She shook her head.

"The first time for me," the old woman said, "was on Thirty-fourth Street about two hundred yards from Fifth Avenue. The reason I know how many yards is because I used to go to business in the garment trade. In my mind, I'm thinking two hundred yards of cloth.

"It was late March, not cold, not warm. The sun was down, but the sky was rosy. A soft pink, a quiet Queen Elizabeth cerise velvet. I stopped to look at some shoes in Altman's window, and am just walking on when I see these two fellows waiting for the light on the corner. They looked all right. To me they didn't seem to be together. They cross the street, one coming to the sidewalk behind me, one in front—nice-looking fellows. Then the one in front says, 'Listen, auntie, give me your money or I'll cut your tits off.' He has the knife in his palm, you see. So what kind of talk is that to talk—on my next birthday, seventy? The other fellow is touching my shoulder. He's behind me. Well, I give them my money quick enough—my watch, thank God only one ring on my hand. My broadtail coat they would have taken—so maybe it's because they didn't have a car, they're afraid of being spotted, two fellows with a fur coat. Listen, they give me the knife here in the cheek, five stitches."

"How terrible," I said.

"Nothing," the old woman said. "The second time was on Seventy-third and Park. My dentist. I was in the hall-way of the eighth floor. This fellow comes up the stairs. He got twenty-five dollars. I'm smarter now. No jewelry second time. He opened the exit door. I fell maybe twenty steps to the landing. Fracture. Compound."

The old woman sighed. "This time," she said, "was at One Hundred Nineteenth and Amsterdam. I was going to a bakery. Special bakery makes these special pastries. My Brooklyn friend loves these pastries. Ricotta filling with melted chocolate streaks. Three fellows, teenagers. They got ten dollars and two subway tokens. My apartment key I got taped inside my shoe. I got no purse with me. In my pocket I got a card with my name for ID."

The old woman reached into her pocket to pull out an index card.

"See?" she said. "I printed my name, but I switched the first and last letters. Where it says T, it says S, and vice-versa. That way if they get the key, they can't look up where I live."

The old woman looked at me, squinting as she focused.

"Where did they get you?" she said.

I held out my hand frosted in white.

"Not where," the old woman said. "Where?"

"Ninety-third and Broadway," I said.

The old woman nodded. "How much did they get?"

"Twelve dollars," I said.

"Good," the old woman said. "That's the right amount for that neighborhood. Seventy-third and Park, I figured

9

twenty-five was right. Got your purse too?"

"No," I said. "I wasn't carrying a purse, just twelve dollars in my pocket."

"Smarts," the old woman said and nodded. "All they got, then?"

"A newspaper," I said. "A tape-recorder. This little cassette-player."

"A cassette-player? You didn't look to me like the kind that carries one of those."

"I use it for notes. The cassette-player," I said. "I dictate into it instead of writing down."

"For notes use paper and pencil. Who steals paper and pencil?"

"Next time," I said.

The old woman leaned forward and looked carefully at the bandaged arm. "Nicked a tendon, did they?"

"What? No, I don't think so. The doctor didn't say that."

"Lucky," the old woman said. She held out her hand. "See this? Butterfly bandage. No stitches. Superficial wound, they call it. Oh, you can learn a lot in ER. Let me tell you something, though. Let me give you some advice. Know why I only needed a butterfly and no stitches? I'll tell you. I dressed just right for the neighborhood. Plain black coat. No purse. But here's the second thing."

The old woman stood up. The policeman stared at her. She ignored him. Facing the bench, she lifted her skirt to just above her knees.

I looked at the old woman's legs. They were surprising, almost shocking—slender and shapely legs, high heels, black suede pumps.

"Yes," the old woman said, acknowledging. "Like Rita Hayworth's. Gorgeous. Me, I'm forty, maybe fifty pounds overweight. But my legs, though, they never change, they always look this good."

The old woman stared sternly at me. "Now pay attention. What you do is jump backwards. It's all in the

10

timing. See, just when the fellows are going like this with the knife, you go like this."

The old woman leaped backwards, her back arched, her arms graceful at her sides, a Pavlova of the ER. She smiled in satisfaction.

"That's the ticket," she said. "Jumping backwards."

The policeman called a name. The T and S were reversed.

"My friend," the old woman said, "has arrived. Take care of yourself." She smoothed down her skirt and leaned over to whisper. "You think because a cop is here that nothing can happen? Something can happen."

"Come on," Grace said. "Hurry! I'm in one of those Emergency Vehicles Only zones."

"Imagine," I said, "they signed me out to you. I've never been signed out to anyone before."

"Yeah," Grace said. "Hurry!"

Grace, called out suddenly, had pulled back her hair with a rubberband. Her face bare of makeup was fresher and softer than I remembered. She tugged nervously at her wraparound skirt where it was drawn dangerously tight across her wide hips. She wore the skirt over brown leotards.

Grace didn't hold the door for me. She was already getting out her car keys.

"No ticket," Grace said. "Thank God! I could feel my heart beating."

"I'm sorry to drag you out," I said formally. Grace was my oldest, although not my best, friend.

"No problem. But let me tell you, I nearly had heart failure being called out of exercise class that way."

"Sorry," I said. "But I remembered you said Wednesday was the day. Exercise class every Wednesday. Two blocks from the hospital, you said." Actually, Grace was always trying to get me to join the class. "You'll love it," Grace had said. "Restorative, trim the waistline, firm the fanny."

11

I didn't need the class.

"Like I always say," Grace said, "what are friends for? Now what happened? You look all right. Mugged, the cop said."

"Yes," I said. Carefully, I rolled the sweater sleeve part-way up. I was embarrassed that Grace might think that she had been called for nothing.

"My God!" Grace said. "Shot?"

"Stabbed."

"My God! Does it hurt much?"

"Like hell," I said. I rolled the sleeve back down. I felt nothing. Throb later, the doctor had said. I had a little paper envelope with Empirin and codeine. Was it possible to be painlessly wounded?

"What did they get?"

"Ninety-third and Broadway."

"What?"

"Oh. About ten, twelve bucks and a tape-recorder."

"My God! Expensive?"

"No," I said. "Cheap. Thirty-nine dollars."

Grace started the motor. She had a brown Chevrolet. She called the car "Hers."

"Let's go, Hers," Grace said. She only spoke to the car in the presence of friends. She leaned forward, inclining her body towards the steering wheel. "Going to tell the children? Don't. It will only frighten them and build in insecurities," she said. She had twin boys.

"Of course I'm going to tell them," I said. "What would I say about the bandages?"

"Tell them you tripped," Grace said. "Fell against a stone wall. Clipped by a bus."

"No," I said.

Grace sighed. She shifted gears. "Easy, Hers," she said. "Children without fathers require special handling, May."

"They have a father."

"Bad image," Grace said, "and not at home. I'm careful with my boys. You know I am. When that creep punched

12

me in the nose, and I had to have the thing reset—did I tell my boys? Absolutely not. I have too much concern for their well-being. A door, I said."

"I'm going to tell the children the truth," I said.

"Well, your funeral. What were you doing walking around with a tape-recorder, anyway?"

"I was making notes," I said. "Thinking about making notes." And they had them now—those two boys. They had my voice. My voice was in someone else's possession. Never let anyone have a part of you, an ancient aunt had once warned me—burn bits of hair, bury snips of nails. Someone had my voice. I had said what ? I had said two whole sentences. They had my two sentences.

Quayle, I am going to get you.
Quayle, I am going to get you.

And the words could appear tomorrow chalked on a sidewalk. Spray-painted on the side of a building, scribbled onto a subway car. Little girls might invent a game for it. *One a Quayle, two a Quayle, three a Quayle, four!*

"I went for a walk," I said. "I just kept walking farther, that's all."

"Walking as catharsis," Grace said. "You should see my therapist. Dr. Morganstern is a creative healer. Here we are. Stop, Hers."

The car balked, coughed, stopped. We were in front of the building where I lived.

"Thanks," I said. "Listen, Grace, I truly, truly appreciate this."

"It's nothing," Grace said. "I'd go in with you, but it's so hard to park, and I don't want Hers to get a ticket."

"I'm all right," I said. "I can manage."

"Right," Grace said. "Call you tomorrow."

"Right," I said.

I got out and gently closed the door. I was suddenly dizzy. Vertigo. Labyrinthitis. In after-shock, I thought. I waited on the sidewalk, even waving until Grace and Hers were out of sight.

I didn't have the apartment key taped to my shoe. I had it buttoned into the breast pocket of my shirt under the sweater. But I didn't pull the key out. I rang the doorbell, and the children opened the door.

My babies, I thought, are they next? Does evil answered by retribution stop at just the mother?

Two

All things can happen. I was considering the commission of a crime. There were fountains from faucets, wire hangers dancing, distant battles. There were criminal tendencies unaccounted for by Empirin and codeine. The envelope seal was unbroken.

The sleeve of the bathrobe had to be adjusted around the bandages. Could I equate my thoughts—breakfast versus crime? Did axe murderers plan their forty whacks in the middle of an ordinary life? The thought had sprung forward in the light of morning, uncoiling from the right hemisphere. I was left-handed. I was considering the committing of a crime—followed by—were there enough eggs for breakfast? Never mind about yesterday, never mind about a vengeful God.

Still, I heeded the old woman's advice. I had a pad of paper and a pencil. *Ninety-five percent of all crimes are domestic in origin,* I wrote.

This one wouldn't be.

But a modern woman's life was no longer so very domestic. Although more of it was than was generally acknowledged.

Eighty-seven percent of all crimes are simple acts of violence, I wrote.

I knotted the belt of the bathrobe. The crime I

contemplated was essentially non-violent. I was not going to do in either my children or my ex-husbands, with whom I still occasionally slept.

Nothing that I was doing—the mixing, the sprinkling of salt—disturbed the thought that was scratching in my mind. It had started with the newspaper. And the television. Even the little radio in the bathroom.

I was completly clean of the charge of domestic violence. Domestic violence? Not now, not if it hadn't been done by the day Harry had left. The three children had stood in the hall keening—Daddy, don't go. They'd stood like pictures of children left out in the rain, wet and streaking. Dickens would have been interested. It hardly mattered that Daddy was scarcely a daddy. Did I do domestic violence? I did not. I ordered the children into the car and drove hastily to Rappaport's. Buy, I said. Pick.

Nothing was left of that day except Leon's red kite. It still existed, tied to a chair in his room. It had never flown. But the significance in that can be downgraded by knowing that Leon collected items of value and gave them permanent immobility.

I willed my arm upward. Plates on the shelf. Plates on the table. When those very same children tramped into the kitchen with their sullen morning spirits, perhaps then the criminal thoughts would depart, ashamed in the white-enamelled gleam of the plain white kitchen where the bacon grease now showered upward. How can you plan a crime while frying bacon, being very careful to make it thoroughly crisp with no soft, moist edges? Trichinosis lurked everywhere, muscular disorders, possible impotence. I guarded against all disease, shuddered at unwarranted blood, kept inoculation records for ready reference.

I was planning a crime. Never mind that it was October, that I lived in New York, that Yom Kippur was hard on our heels, and that my children and I had reversed moods, that I was the foul one in the morning now.

The pattern of behavior that I had once named "movement memory" permitted the performance of all morning tasks despite internal confusion. Thus, I poured, I sliced, I placed.

Crimes of excess made the newspapers. Husbands invaded suburban love-nests. Excess, excess, excess. It was commonly believed that scenes of revealed passion occurred with music of another decade and with sips of wine. Confession, tears, reconciliation. Actually, seventy percent of all discoveries of passion were made in the kitchen. The light would be particularly unshadowed, everything with a thick Gauguin-black line around it. Harry sitting in the kitchen, for example. He had a freshly made cup of coffee. The very air was coffee-scented. The children had left for school. May, he said, there is this girl. As if to absorb more information, opening myself, I pushed a fingernail into my palm. This girl, he said.

He yearned for her. This girl was three months past twenty-something. This girl was tight-muscled, witty, possessed of a Cossack's aggressive streak.

When Harry spoke, I was well-rehearsed. Four friends had been in similar circumstances. He tells you, you cry, he cries. Never, he promises. And then for a long time you carefully check the clock, the calendar, who is where.

Her hair, Harry said. Yes, that must be it. Her hair is the exact shade of yours when we met. Ripe wheat.

"Out," I said.

But essentially the scene was non-violent. No coffee thrown, no dispersal of shards, no ceremonial rending of the clothes.

I made the toast. With the Harry thing, I could turn to a proper confessor, but who could I turn to now? With a thing like this, you realize the shallowness, the small-time limits of previous confessions. I could speak to friends about Harry, about the girl, about her grey silk dress. But with this thing, could I call Grace to say, "Good morning, my friend, I am planning to embark upon an unlawful act."

"May, are you crazy? It's your arm. Retaliation is no panacea. Think about the children. The cops. My God, you will be caught! The newspapers. Mother trapped in crime-wave sweep."

"One crime, Grace."

"You are too much by yourself, May. Too much in the company of children. You should get out. Mingle, try. And you shouldn't let Harry spend the night. Brought the children back late, long drive across town—how can you believe that? Do you sleep with him? Do you do it?"

"All I would need is one crime, Grace. If properly planned."

No, at that point Grace would hang up. She would call Huldie and Rosemary, and then the three of them would come over. They would harangue, discuss, remember ghosts, cloud the perfect simplicity of the issue.

I could do it this way. I could call Grace and say, "Listen, I am considering blackmailing someone."

Grace would roll over, clutch tighter the white telephone with the long, long extension cord. She would be in bed, her reserves of flesh loosely hanging from her, a style she'd worn since schooldays.

"Blackmail?" Her lips would part, moist, exuberant. "Someone I know?"

I would say no.

Was it conceivable I could know someone she didn't?

"Who? What?"

The who I'd tell her. The what, no.

"Quayle."

"Quayle? I don't know any Quayle."

"I do." The newspapers do. The television does, the radio does.

"You know a secret? May, do you know a secret?"

My mother always said they're going to come and get

you if you don't keep your secrets. She was, however, speaking about politics.

"Yes," I would say. "I know a secret."

The children were sitting at the table with the bacon and the toast and the eggs. Brown-haired children, blue-eyed children, children that frowned at the morning light. Joanne pushed back her hair until it was stored behind each ear. She was pretty at sixteen—but short. This suggested a vulnerability not real.

"I don't feel like going to school this year," she said.

I sighed, yet about certain things I was implacable. "No," I said.

"Molly isn't going. Molly is taking a year off."

"Molly is seventeen," I said.

"Molly is sixteen."

"Molly is seventeen," I said. "I know she is. Her mother told me."

Certain lies came very easily to me. Perhaps worse crimes might come just as easily. Anyway, this Molly had already left the city. She went away to find herself.

"Next year, then," Joanne said, looking past the table to where the future might be, outside the window.

Richard was also annoyed. He mumbled about scheduling. I must listen. Wasn't he mumbling about scheduling? Two sports conflicted. He hated both. Richard was strong and sturdy. Maybe Harry looked like Richard looks when Harry was twelve.

Leon didn't want to go to school, either. He never wanted to do anything Joanne didn't want to do.

"Not today," I said. "Joanne is not speaking about not going to school today."

I too looked beyond the table to the window. How bad was a crime if you didn't hurt anyone? I drank the coffee. But someone must be hurt. There'd be a person being blackmailed. Did it matter if he deserved it? Sexual. Everyone would automatically assume that the secret was

18

sexual. Quayle photographed in bed with three women. Not enough for the times. Three old women. Quayle accused of having male lovers. Quayle's house revealed to be den of the unspeakable—straps, whips, truly strange contraptions.

But no, it was nothing like that.

There was noise. The whine of the elevator or a distant bus. The children leaped at the sounds. They grabbed things, yelled, pushed. Mother was forgotten. Our debates were forgotten. They were on the way, cries of "Shut up!" Too late I noticed the traces of milk outlining Leon's mouth. I had been negligent in my duties. No one had stopped to kiss my cheek, to bid the provider good-bye. Everyone was in a hurry.

They were gone.

If you had a real job, May.

That was always implied. I had a *real* job. Never mind if no one understood it. I supported the three children, the apartment—I alone put the coffee in the cup. Harry meant to help. But Harry lacked success. When I threw him out, he had his clothes. He came back a week later, his gestures studied, pathetic. "I need the car," he said. "What can I do? How can I get around? I am lost, May."

I gave him the car. A car purchased by me. You are a fool, my friends said. Was he grateful? Do you think that he will be grateful?

But wasn't I supposed to be thinking about Quayle? I might as well have had Grace and Huldie and Rosemary at the table. We were all friends from childhood. We had known each other so long we didn't even have to like each other anymore. This is what has happened, we said to each other. And sometimes we even listened to each other.

Grace and Huldie and Rosemary could have been sitting around my table—drinking my coffee. And telling me that if I had a real job, if I went out into the real world, I would not be considering what I was considering.

19

Blackmail.
One big kill.

The room where I did my work was an alcove off the living room. It was at a right angle to the living room. All the apartments in the line marked "C" on the builder's plans have this alcove. In most apartments, this space was a place for pleasure. A family room, the renting agent said, a den, a rathskeller, etc., etc. When the children went to other apartments to see friends, they came back with tales of the alcoves. Televisions there, bars, couches. But in our alcove there was a formica table on steel legs, file cabinets, shelves, a door. Pleasure was elsewhere.

Still in my bathrobe, still in my pain, thinking of my plan, I entered my alcove to sit and reconnoitre. I hadn't seen Quayle for at least seven years. The exact dates were in a notebook. I never followed their careers once I'd finished my work for them. Why should I? But Quayle would remember me, wouldn't he? Even if my clients were so often unable to accept exactly what had happened, wouldn't Quayle be the exception?

I didn't need my notes on him. Not yet. For one thing, I remembered Quayle's apartment that first time. The maid had opened the door. Later, the wife had stepped into the room interrupting. She wore a yellow hat. "I'm going out," she said. Quayle had made the introduction, and then he had dismissed the woman with a wave. Annoyed, slightly annoyed.

Afterwards, there was never anyone to greet me. My arrivals and my departures were unattended except by Quayle. Our appointments were held on Saturday afternoons. I went to his apartment—he came to the door, we went to the room where we did our work.

The first time though, it was the maid that opened up to me. I was expected. "This way," the maid had said. Quayle's room. There was a splash of Aubusson rug of excellent quality on the floor. I recognized the period and

20

design from a previous job. Quayle's desk stood before a wall of rosewood shelves, small lighted niches where bits of abstract sculpture were placed. Black, curved stones. A copy of a Pre-Columbian statue of the God of Complex Emotions. Did Quayle know that it wasn't authentic? I didn't tell him.

Quayle himself was one of those men with black and silver hair. His appearance was handsome and comforting. He removed his dark-rimmed glasses from time to time and rubbed rhythmically at the bridge of his nose. But I could never see the cause—perhaps a parasitic infection. Often he leaned forward and nodded. I could imagine sitting across from such a man and telling him about separations, desertions, refusals.

I had a legal pad and two pens. I waited, observing all rules of etiquette. My role was always that. Quayle smiled. He was definitely at ease and in harmony with the world. I, on the other hand, had taken a train and a bus, raincoat wrinkled from arduous travel.

"I'll come to the point," Quayle said.

My pen was poised.

"I have been planning a publication for the last few years. I have in mind a piece about some theories. An expansion of my work and thoughts. This has been suggested to me by many people."

I looked up. Quayle made a steeple with the tips of his fingers. His silver-edged hair curled to the tops of his ears. I noticed that he sucked imported candies, popped lavender, bullet-shaped pastilles into his mouth.

"Book-length," he said.

It was a quiet room, deadened by plaster and leather and velvet. I waited for the draperies of his mind to unfold. By nature I am not assertive. During this gap in our activities, I calculated the size of my fee. Big. As the silence expanded, I struggled against certain urges.

"The subject?" I finally said. It was at this point that the last dollar calculation was always made. By the time

Quayle came along, I was experienced, I understood. I had a formula.

Quayle turned his head towards the window.

I could see that his lips were dry and cracked. Quayle withered and shrivelled in front of me.

"Perhaps," I said, "we can work together on defining the theories. We'll base them on your interests."

Quayle capitulated at once. He smiled, but not broadly, a secretive, slight smile.

"In my files," he said and opened a drawer of his desk. "Yes, you may have this."

He handed me a one-page account of his life. I folded the sheet and placed it with the pad of paper into my folder. Then I stated my fee.

"That," Quayle said. "That."

In truth, he winced.

I nodded and waited. He would, I knew, pay. The sum was not in any way unreasonable. There was my time, my research, my reputation—my references.

He stood up, the deal made by implication, the interview concluded. We shook hands, and I stared into the clear blue of his eyes.

He had one stipulation that I heard often. "I am not accustomed," he said, "to having my employees discuss my affairs."

"No," I said, his newest employee. "Certainly not."

I still had my original notes, the material that I had checked, and my interpretations. It had actually been quite easy, at least as far as my relations with my client. Quayle was not much for conferences. When there was a great deal of input from the client, it was more difficult.

The book was finished on time. But then, I never missed a deadline. A matter of pride. A year later there had been another one, this time his collected essays, *Permissible Love-play*—also the fruit of my secret labors.

What had happened to Quayle? He had left the city.

Hadn't I read that? An endowed chair elsewhere. I had never thought about him again. That was customary. Although some former clients would write to me, I never replied. The success of my book is stunning, they would write. My work was received with kudos, they would write.

To these adoptive parents claiming the agonies of birth, I sent no further words. Interaction with my clients ended when they paid me. And it was that way with Quayle. Two assignments and then all exchange between us had come to a halt, stopped.

But today, this very day, guess what? A work of significance, said the newspaper, a work of genius. And so said the television and the radio.

By Quayle—my Quayle, my Quayle—Quayle of the clear blue eyes.

Quayle had won the Nobel Prize!

Three

Let me tell you how it started, this work that I do, this occupation that earns your Quayle a Nobel Prize.

I was a helper. I was employed by the firm of Eberham & Earling. I was married to a man named Benjamin. No alcove back in those days. I shared office space with an Alice and a Helen. Helen assisted a vice-president, and Alice and I assisted anyone who needed assistance. So one day Ernest Eberham's cousin Sanford was hovering around my desk. In those times this was permissible— much has changed since. Even his form of address. "Cupcake," he said. "I have been told that you can put together sentences."

I nodded.

23

"Well now, cupcake," Sanford Eberham said, "what I need is a nice little talk for Friday."

"What?" I said. My manner was so respectful that I may even have ducked my head.

"On what?" he said. "On synthetic material. On the future of synthetic material."

"What kind?"

He looked at me with disbelief. "Cloth," he said. "Synthetic. Are you sure that you can handle this?"

"Certainly," I said. I had experience with the ersatz. I'd seen plenty of it.

"Treat him right," Helen said after Sanford Eberham departed from our area. Perhaps she'd seen him pat me on the head.

Benjamin was having a hard time. Benjamin was an artist. We slept on a pull-out couch in the living room. The linoleum did not have a pattern. Benjamin used the bedroom for his work. He was in his room staring at a canvas when I came home and explained about the assignment.

"Sound's like extra work. Doesn't it sound like extra work?"

I nodded. I had carried home nine books from the library, there were three rooms to clean, dinner to prepare.

"Not related to Eberham and Earling, is it? Doesn't sound like it is."

"No," I said. "I spoke to the right secretary. Sanford Eberham is looking for a new job. It's a speech before a group of manufacturers."

"Charge him," Benjamin said.

"You mean extra?"

"Extra."

I made dinner. Suppose they fired me? What would we live on? I worked all evening on the speech. I made notations in the margins where Sanford Eberham should pause. Look at your audience, I wrote. Lick your lips. I started off with a jest about a fellow in a suit and it's real wool and it itches. The speech was ready by Wednesday. I called it "From Polyester to Infinity."

"Terrific," Sanford Eberham said. "A work of art."

I cleared my throat. "Extra," I said.

"What?"

"Extra. Unless you want me to charge it on my time sheet as overtime."

From Sanford Eberham's own personal account I received a check for two hundred dollars.

"You see," Benjamin said as he took the check.

From this acorn, a mighty oak. More assignments.

"Regard it as an avocation," Benjamin said. "I'll buy you a special table, a special lamp. For in the corner of the bedroom."

The new work took a lot of time, and I considered leaving Eberham & Earling.

"Too risky," Benjamin said. "Wait."

And he went out evenings to give me peace. Grace reported seeing him in line for a movie on Third Avenue.

"May," Grace said, "the woman he was with was radiant. A knockout. He's a bastard. Where did he find her? A bastard. Handsome, though."

Huldie reported it differently.

"In a restaurant," she said. "The woman was all right, but nothing special."

Perhaps it wasn't the same woman.

Rosemary sent over a locksmith. "Be sensible," she said. It was a time of first husbands for all of us.

I changed the lock.

Most of my work was clear-cut and aboveboard. My clients were pleased. They introduced me around. "My little writer helper," they said. And then with a twinkle and a pat—"The woman in my life. She puts my ideas on paper."

The fees got bigger, and the work more confidential. I

was ushered into back rooms, met in hallways. "My typist," they said when intercepted. "We're having a love affair," one explained, whispering of motels in New Jersey.

Quayle wasn't from this time. Quayle was from later. And through it all my silence was always assured, my perfect discretion. If my friends were to be asked, they would say, "We know everything about May. Don't we know everything about May? We have known everything about May since May got her first bra."

How had I kept my secret? I followed advice—my mother's advice—a secret is best kept by keeping it exposed. My secret was out in the open. No locked drawers, no bolted doors. Out in the open where everyone could see it—the books, the papers, the notes. Even my personal file system. Three shoe-boxes filled with index cards, the boxes on a shelf. Nothing was locked up. Who noticed pinpricks on the card, some on the left, some on the right—certain words underlined?

Several years ago, during the time of Quayle, things were difficult. Harry was selling miniature space stations. I had been called to school because Joanne had been caught reading dirty French poetry, and Richard had temporarily run away.

Harry had always referred to my efforts as Mother's Work. "It's like a hobby," he told his friends. I permitted this, I didn't object, I smiled. Who would have guessed that what I did was our bread and butter?

The arm hurt, and I pulled down the second shoebox with pain. There was just one other client under "Q." Quayle's card had three pinpricks on the right. I pondered the significance of that. Sometimes I switched the code, sometimes I couldn't remember. I tried to concentrate. I focused on the peeling paint on the windowsill. There was a need for haste. I knew that. This wasn't an affair that could wait. Speed was necessary.

"Never delay," my mother had always said. "To delay

is stupid." But hadn't abortion been the subject?

I took a piece of paper and wrote BLACKMAIL. What should I ask for? 1) Entire prize. 2) Monthly retainer. 3) Both.

He had the prize money, he had his salary, he had his fees. He had my fame—a license forever!

I decided to research the subject. I would order a computerized ten-year search of all newspaper articles about Quayle and family. I'd mark off all pertinent articles to read. There would be microfiches to use—I needn't worry about the destruction of newsprint. Dun & Bradstreet to check. Banks. Investments. The works.

What was I going to do?

I was going to blackmail the son of a bitch!

I prepared for the initial contact. From the morning newspaper I had learned the city where he now lived, the name of his university. I got the telephone number from the operator. It was the number of his department at the university. As expected, his home telephone was unlisted.

The woman who answered the phone was cheerful, excited. "The phone is ringing off the wall," she said.

"I can imagine," I said. "My I speak to Dr. Quayle?"

"Oh no," the woman said. Was her good humor based on answering his telephone? "He's not here. Are you a member of the press?"

"An old friend," I said. "An old friend calling to wish him well. I'd like him to return the call."

Yes, I certainly would. This old friend certainly would. And today, please.

"We're promising nothing," the woman said. "But I'll add your message to our list."

"Thank you," I said.

It was done. Begun. I felt, I decided, exactly like a criminal. My heart was pounding, my breath coming in snorts, skin damp, my thoughts a knot.

I'll never be able to carry it off. I have been too long

living alone, too much in this room. They were right. I should try Grace's therapist.

I will deny your existence, Quayle will say. In his hands will be the work of significance, *Eine Leerstelle*.

Guess who's in your book, I will reply to the son of a bitch.

Quayle's eyebrows of pale silver will descend with his big-shot frown.

In my book?

Yes, in your book, idiot.

Who?

My mother.

Your mother?

My mother. Also, my Aunt Giselle.

The dumbfuck will faint, clatter from his chair in the presence of unbearable truths.

Four

To whom can you tell the story of your life? For instance, I grew up in a Socialist household. The family was everywhere, but mainly we're talking about Sonya the mother, Giselle an aunt, Trasker a sort of uncle. There was a lot of sharing that was very tiring. I wanted at one time a pair of Shirley Temple shoes with ankle straps. No one thought that was a thing worth wanting.

To unburden yourself of these memories would awaken such a sense of relief—and no penance. To be able to do so in the presence of a compassionate nature and tell how it was perceived. The immensities, the leap of acceptance, the subterranean hatreds, the recanting.

It was in the evening, grey light, the gloom of nostalgia. I had put my head on Benjamin's shoulder and my arms around his waist. "My childhood," I began, "was a troubled time. My mother was politically active. All the mothers of my friends were politically active, but my mother was the worst. We had a press in the basement, men with knapsacks at the door. Once we drove all night to the Canadian border."

Benjamin always stopped me on the way. "Sure, baby," he interrupted. He kissed my shoulder and moved me backwards, skillfully aiming me at the bedroom. I never got to the part where Sonya, walking on the banks of the Mississippi, dropped her sack and Huck jumped in after it. "I can get it myself," Sonya had yelled, her feet sinking into the mud.

One June day I began to Harry, "My mother chained herself to a factory door between two brick posts. A terrible strike, they threw bottles, rocks. Pictures in the newspapers. I was a girl, a child. I was frightened, humiliated."

"Look at this," Harry said. "I think this will sell. Calculators that work with a stylus, no batteries, a calculating abacus."

Were the others better?

"No," Grace said.

"Absolutely not," said Huldie.

Rosemary shook her head.

"We were there. It was not like that." They linked arms.

"For goodness sakes, Mother," Joanne said.

How did my reputation grow? I was passed on from one person to another. Sometimes, they sold my name. "She'll turn out a suitable piece of work," they said.

It remained a question of beginnings. For instance, the time I was seduced by a physiological occurrence. There was that shadowy movement on the left in the farthest range of my peripheral vision. If I turned my head too quickly in that direction, the shape, although it was more amorphous than shape connotes, remained, even expanded as the wings dried. The color was that of twilight. It was changeable, in a state of evolving. The colors of twilight being blue, grey, grey-black, even pink to orange. First the shadow annoyed me, and there was much rubbing of the eye, much brushing away of hair. Then, presently, I was possessed by fear. What could happen? An ophthalmic aberration, the prelude to a blinding disease, a prodrome of darkness.

"Harry," I said and curled against his body, "I'm afraid. I am losing my vision, my mind."

"No, baby," he said, "you're just seeing things."

I tried to conquer my terror. I reread the place where Beowulf came ashore to rid the land of terror. "Watch out," Giselle shouted just as Grendel was about to attack. Beowulf had her to thank, the dope.

Then, absurdly, I realized that I had grown fond of the shadow in my eye, coming as it did at five in the evening and leaving promptly at about seven. Some days before my appointment to have my eyes examined, the shadow disappeared.

I had lunch with Huldie. "I feel as if I have lost something," I said.

Huldie shrugged. "You mean like a purse?"

"A companion," I said.

"I don't know why you don't want a nice office job," Huldie said. "Someplace to go where you are welcomed."

Harry was considering bankruptcy when I received a telephone call from a man who had just returned from a trip to New Guinea.

"Up the fee," Harry whispered. "Things are tight all over."

"May Alto," S.R. said, "I would like your assistance on a real sweetheart of a job. I have just returned from a splendid trip, and I must have a permanent record."

30

We met on the Lexington Avenue side of Bloomingdale's. S.R. had gone to New Guinea to collect butterflies, and although he was an amateur, he had a reputation for pursuit. The book would be called *Butterfly Adventures in New Guinea.*

S.R. was carrying a shopping bag. "In here," he said, "a copy of my itinerary, some butterfly books to be returned when through, and my excellent photographs. The best, of course, were purchased in New Guinea."

That S.R. was no quibbler, and we settled business matters swiftly. I rubbed my hands with the fine dust of butterfly wings and went to work.

I took S.R. through the rain forest, mythically dark and primitive, gave him several amusing conversations with a former naval officer now following the life cycle of the bird of paradise, allowed S.R. a few days of unexplained fever—chills, aching head, flashing lights. Then I sent him butterfly hunting, past butterflies that favor carrion to an excellent specimen of *Ornithoptera priamus.* S.R. admired a fritillary and made his way to the Gulf of Carpentaria.

Don't think that I had forgotten the shadow. I yearned for its presence, mysterious and soothing. And it did not desert me. When the lawyer told Harry bankruptcy was out of the question, the shadow was reborn as a twilit butterfly.

S.R. stood in a field knee-high with man-planted grasses, the wind sounding. *The wind,* I gave him to write, *reminded me of carillons, of a twelve-tone piece. It was then that I saw a small butterfly moving as some do on the waves of early night. A delicate creature with wings indented in a U-shaped scroll. I could not with that brief glimpse identify it. Yet it seemed to me to be the reason for seeking butterflies,* I let him continue, *the moment of civilized beauty.*

The following evening at approximately the same time, S.R. went again into the field. He stood there alone, waiting. The butterfly appeared, its wings wide. He saw only one butterfly of this type. *I was prepared*, he wrote. *I gave chase. The butterfly escaped me. I never saw that butterfly again, yet it remained in my memory. A butterfly whose exact color I am unable to report, the vagaries of the light. I think perhaps there was a white patch on the fore-wing. I have named the butterfly* Gisellasia traskius.

"I like that," S.R. said. He was a jovial man. The book was not expected to make a stir, but he was pleased. "Good touch, fine butterfly."

"Yes," I said. "Pay attention now. If you come across anything about your book, a review, comments from your friends, see if they mention *Gisellasia traskius*. Report if they have ever seen it."

"Right," he said. "They might have. Fine butterfly. What's it called again?"

"Look it up," I said. "Page seventy-three."

At all times I tried to be a good mother and to bring my children into the life that I led. She's always in the house, I'd heard them complain. They could do so little unheard.

"I've been doing some research on butterflies," I said at the dinner table. "In fact, I have the very book here."

"I don't care about butterflies," Joanne said.

"Bugs," Richard said.

"Old girl," Harry said, "I'm not much for the birds and the bees—at least not the real ones."

There I was with the book, the right glossy pages flagged. At my insistence, there was a line drawing of *Gisellasia traskius*. It hadn't turned out right though. It looked too much like a butterfly.

In the spring Harry was still in the apartment. Leon got the measles and wanted only butterscotch pudding to eat. The refrigerator, Joanne said, made her puke. It was full of yellow stuff.

I was thinking about beginnings all during that period, but I wasn't tormented by them. It was simply my need to overcome early training in order and sequence. The one that was supposed to be followed by the two. It was the all-things-in-their-own-time concept. I never did agree with that. Nor did I have any traffic with predestination. If Clyde Griffiths had gone out that night with Giselle, would Roberta have drowned? It was merest happenstance that had made Giselle late, that had made Clyde think that he'd been stood up, that had caused that particular American Tragedy.

"Where is he?" Giselle said. She was on the right corner. He could have waited half an hour.

It was the prospect of doing the Secretary's autobiography that had me blocked for a week. "Do you remember," I asked Grace, "that time when we were kids and the police chased us from the demonstration and arrested our mothers? Do you remember the officer who came to the house? That very fat man in the grey fedora?"

"No," Grace said. "I wasn't there."

"Yes," I said, "and we were terrified."

"No," Grace said.

"You were there," I said. "You ran for help. Huldie kicked the man."

"No," Grace said.

I took the shuttle to Washington. The Secretary met me in an apartment in Chevy Chase. The Secretary tried to squeeze my knee, but I withdrew that body part. "Business," I said.

We spent some time deciding what years to use. "My boyhood," the Secretary said. "It's risky to go beyond my boyhood. I refer to the period as 'Growing Up on the Prairie.' Nice?"

I was making notes. If we moved the boyhood up three years, that would allow for the inclusion of a rather historically important State Fair.

"Good thinking," the Secretary said. "Give them a lot of that crap. The less personal, the better. Go easy on the folks too. The father owned a general store. I don't know too much about the mother."

I made the father a seller of farm implements. The mother was renowned for her plum preserves. It seemed best to presage the Secretary's later leadership in agrarian reforms. There were the one-room schoolhouse, the winter snow-storms, the graduations.

The Secretary had actually spoken at his graduation. "High collar, tight suit, the usual," he said. "Loved it. Loved the sound of my voice, all those people staring up." He didn't remember what he had said.

I wrote him a fresh graduation speech. And then I stuck in Giselle.

Actually, I had never really liked Giselle. But at that time I was a child, and she embarrassed me. She was noticed even in the clutter of our house. She was sent to us, shipped to us. Away from purges, away from trouble. I suspected that they wanted to be rid of her.

"She'll share your room," my mother said. "Temporary."

I was ten, and I didn't like it. "She never combs her hair," I said. "She took the whole closet. She sings in the morning. She's not even a real aunt."

"Endure the people," my mother said.

Imagine Giselle, a cockscomb of ribbons on top of her fuzzy hair, a rasping song in a foreign tongue, a menace, a public one. Everyone saw her. "Hey," they yelled. "Look at who May's got! A loony croony!"

But Giselle wasn't afraid like other newcomers. She went for walks in the neighborhood, out of the neighborhood. She never got lost. It was June, and she discovered graduations. Giselle started wearing white dresses, flowing robes. She followed people into auditoriums. Sometimes, she'd follow them to weddings.

"Graduations are beautiful," Giselle told me when she got into my only white slip.

"Balls," I said.

"My Aunt Giselle," I said to Harry in his time.
"Who?" Harry had said.
"Giselle. You know."
No, he didn't.

After I completed the Secretary's graduation speech, I checked ancient train schedules in the library. There was always a reader who knew train schedules.

I remember, wrote the Secretary, *that on a hot day bereft of wind the train brought Giselle to Lincoln, Nebraska.*

She was spending the summer in the house of the Secretary's nearest neighbors. She wore a white muslin dress at the graduation. A beautiful day. About the same age as the future Secretary, Giselle was dark-haired, pixie-like. She and the Secretary had many long, joyous talks that summer, meeting beneath the shelter of the single oak on the lawn of his parents' house. Giselle at sixteen was a student of Bukanov, and although her theories about land-reform were too radical for the young future Secretary, nevertheless he listened to her with the open mind of youth.

It was an interesting opportunity, he later said, *to find out these different views. And from such a charming person.*

What went on at the back of the house? Away from the windows, by the shed. Did Giselle advocate free love? Did she have an abortion? How responsible a person was the Secretary?

"Nothing through the mails," the Secretary had said.

I flew back to Washington and delivered the manuscript. I spent the night at a hotel anxiously waiting to find out what the Secretary thought about *Growing Up on the Prairie: My Life and the Land.*

We met the next afternoon in a dining room of a Ramada Inn. "May I kiss you in appreciation?" the Secretary said. I didn't step back fast enough.

35

"I am terribly pleased," he said. "You have captured my essence."

"Thank you," I said.

"You want to celebrate?" the Secretary said. "What say we celebrate, little lady?"

"No," I said.

All the details were recorded in the pinpricks on the cards. Also, there were the underlined words, and a Xerox copy of the Secretary's check. He'd signed it himself.

"We have a relative," I told the children, "who had an interesting association with a member of the current federal government."

They were watching television. They were watching a movie about killing. Everyone was in a good mood. "Later, Mother," they said.

"In this book," I said. "I'll leave it on the table. There is a bookmark flagging the right place."

I tore off a piece of newspaper to mark the place. I draped a strand of hair across the cover. Two days later, I removed the hair and put the book away.

Yes, parts passed unnoticed, even today.

Take *The Castle*, for instance, where—at one of the turnings in the road or more correctly, in the maze—K. failed to heed Sonya's cry "Come, follow me." He assumed the cry to be different than it actually was—although it was plainly stated on that page in that edition of the book—"Come, follow me to the Castle." But K. neglected to hear the last three words.

No, I've chosen the wrong word—not hear but see. What did he *see*—or the reader? What had they *seen* later in that newspaper? It was a childhood prank. I can't say that it was sublimated. I had never even tried to tell Benjamin.

It came back because of a dream, returned from memory storage. In this dream, I say, "Mother, Mother, I can't stand this life." And Mother says, "You must. It's all there is." Then I woke up with no problem with orientation, because my mother would never have said that. She would have said, "Don't philosophize. Be a doer!"

It began at the round table where there was tea and cake and strong opinions were being shouted. I was annoyed because, as often happened, the place at the table that I considered to be mine was taken by someone else. I was evicted if a strange grownup needed a chair. "Stand, little one," I was told. Eat from a distance, listen from a distance.

I left the room. Did I tell you in the cellar we had a printing press? No big thing—old, noisy. My mother wrote these pamphlets. Her most recent one was there in pencil, waiting to be set in type. I read the opening line. *Fifty percent of the world's oppressed* was how the sentence started.

That's what *she* thought. I took a sheet of paper and counted everyone upstairs—family, visitors, strangers. I did some mathematics. Seven percent was me. I erased. I amended. I forged. *Seven percent of the world's oppressed* . . .

I never regarded my changes in a text as a sign of some need to interfere. Never did I see them as a surrender of my interest in my past. Nor did I suppose it was foolish to risk my livelihood as I doubtlessly did. And now this, now Quayle.

Hurray!

There were many times during our marriage, both before and after Harry's attempts to open an adults-only store, when he would come home at two in the afternoon and we would lock ourselves in the bedroom and do it. These were the times of spiritual weakness.

"Harry," I would suggest, "let's go on a spree."

But he would say, "You have an assignment. Don't forget the kids' tuition."

I would get up and put on my clothes. He was right.

There was always work to do. In my alcove I would examine my latest assignment. I did not treat all material in the same way. A study of the geology of a desert, the chemistry of Neptune, the confessions of an indiscreet madam—some I just left alone. When I put something in—Mother and Trasker at Barkham Manor when the Piltdown man was uncovered—it was right, it was in keeping. They belonged.

Yes, occasionally I wondered if I dared too much, and there were episodes of nausea and unsettling moods. "A woman must adjust," my mother had said.

I was scrupulous in my use of history, careful of technology. It was not paradoxical that what I added illustrated and made clearer. I adjusted.

For instance, there were the diaries of a certain survivor. I'm not mentioning any names. Gulags and so forth and so on. We called it *A Day in the Life* of someone or other, who remembers? Anyway, it was a rather straightforward account with a scattering of literary allusions along with my customary genius for characters in crisis.

Take that strange and baffling description of Sonya unexpectedly seized by a certain agony as the result of a violent movement of the arm and leg. The pain, sharp and nearly incapacitating, was not thought to be psychosomatic in origin, although her two marriages and financial uncertainties were considered. When she moaned, the nurses bent over her. "What's that?" they said. "Did you hear?" "Ivan." "Didn't she say Ivan?"

Sonya shared a room with two other women. "You probably have a tumor," the woman named Alice told Sonya. "Do you have morning headache?" the one named Helen asked. Sonya didn't reply. Someone sent roses to her at the clinic. She recovered—her pain went into remission. She left. Later, one of the nurses saw her again. "Isn't this her?" The other nurses bent over to look. It was a photograph of five people and the King of the Belgians.

I went out one evening to a small Italian restaurant with Grace and Huldie. We were being festive to cheer up Grace. Her nose had been broken and reset. Now she disliked the new one.

"I look strange?" she kept asking.

"You don't," I said.

"Look the same," Huldie said.

"The same? I wanted to look better. I asked to look better."

"Better," I said. "We meant better."

We all ordered pasta. "Al dente," I said, "with cheese and butter and five cloves of gently sauteed garlic."

"Are you alone all the time?" Grace said. "Now that Harry's gone, don't you see anyone?"

I shook my head.

Huldie sighed and sipped some wine. "I'd like to make an introduction," she said. "You'll like him. My former brother-in-law."

"No," I said.

"It's a period of mourning," Grace explained. "May is going through a period of mourning."

"He's been divorced Two *years*," Huldie said.

Huldie and I once wore identical red-and-blue plaid dresses. Our mothers had bought them from a pedlar. A special deal for two. We hated them. The Jailbird Twins, we were called. But Huldie was smarter. Huldie climbed a fence and tore hers, ripped it, ravelled the edges. A rag, her mother said. A rag.

"He's not fresh from anyone," Huldie said. "Do you understand the significance of that?"

"I prescribe a job," Grace said. "Don't I always tell you that? A nice get-up-in-the-morning-and-get-dressed-and-go-out job."

We ate our spaghetti. Huldie told us about her new job. "I hate it," she said. "The boss is a lousy person."

*

How My Mother Spends Her Day.

It was an assignment.

"You can take either parent," Joanne had said. "You have a choice."

My mother, Joanne wrote in the fifth grade, does not have a job. But she earns money. She stays home all day and reads and types, except when she goes to the library. Daddy is into industrial production.

"For God's sake, Joanne," I said.

After the children left for school, I always washed and dressed, even put on lipstick. Then I checked my calendar. I never missed an appointment. I worked in my office, my alcove, until one o'clock. Among the libraries that I used were the Forty-second Street branch of the New York Public Library, also the Midtown Reference Library, the Pierpoint Morgan Library, the Ford Foundation library, and the New York Academy of Sciences library.

I wrote all this down and gave it to Joanne.

"Too late," she said. "I already turned in my paper."

"Next time it comes up," I said.

"All right," Joanne said. "But it doesn't sound like what anyone else does."

My work was not secret.

"Secrets are dangerous," Mother had said. "Keep them in the open."

So I did.

This was well expressed in *Princess Daisy*. That daughter of Prince Stash Valensky, the White Russian polo player, had a secret about her childhood—didn't Giselle figure in that?

Some secrets were neat, tight, everything fitted together as in a swell who-dun-it. Others were sloppy. For example, I balanced Harry's checkbook. That explained several telephone calls. Also, Harry had nibbled at the tuition account. We needed more money.

I thought about *La Comédie humaine*—not a

coincidence—because another life of Balzac came along just then. Mrs. A.T. was a nice woman who was anxious to make her mark. There was a sabbatical, notes, papers, a grant. I liked her, a fluttery little woman.

As was my custom before the lives of all novelists, I reread Balzac. Once again there was that lousy human condition, and I was much moved by the account of Père Goriot and his heartless daughters.

This led me to the philosophy of Swedenborg. I tried to understand Balzac's interest in deciphering the connections between fate and the temporal view of man, the themes of light and darkness. If old Goriot had been a nobleman or had at least possessed a facade of nobility, would his fashionable daughters have deserted him?

It all came down to physical appearance and destiny. I would therefore create an appendix to Mrs. A.T.'s study of Balzac and put in the tale of Giselle cross-referenced to approximately 1835, with four detailed footnotes. What the hell. I have always believed that this chronological order thing was overrated. As Mother said, "The right place comes if you keep your eye out for it."

"What do you think?" I asked Mrs. A.T. We were sitting in a booth in a luncheonette on Broadway. I was afraid that the icy blasts from the air-conditioner would chill Mrs. A.T. She wasn't young.

"Not cold at all," she assured me. "Here's the check. You have made excellent use of my scholarly material. You have captured my ideas."

"I thought so," I said.

I showed a library edition of the book to Grace. She read the marked passages.

"That's nice," she said. "Tell me, if I wore a strand of pearls with my black silk, would I look too old? I mean, would I look extremely middle-aged?"

"Yes," I said. "Wear white."

"White?"

"White. And get yourself some shoes with ankle straps."

I added this book to the other volumes on my special shelves. I have shelves and shelves for these books. I have always fought off any urges to catalogue. My selections are pulled from a larger repository; they explain, correct, assist, state the truth as it appeared to have happened. I placed the newest life of Balzac between *The Canterbury Tales* and *Of Time and the River*.

So you can see that I was quite experienced when Quayle appeared on the scene. The direction of my work had been set. By the time Quayle showed up, I was well into it. There were many books on those shelves. All before Quayle. There were books of every kind—science, finance, all the arts, not to mention fiction and poetry for those who so required. I was confident. I was competent. I was great and inspired.

Five

If Quayle didn't call back within twenty-four hours, I decided to regard it as an omen, an augury of potential difficulties. But of course he would call. What else could he do? I had only to wait. To wait and plan.

I had seen his photograph, the patrician profile profiled. There he was in the *Times,* solemn and wise. The dirty bastard. It occurred to me to add some crayon touches—horns, the goatee. But that was a child's revenge. I'd have none of that. It wasn't easy waiting for what I wanted. My alcove, the very apartment, was impossible. How could I spend the day anticipating the ring of the telephone? It was out of the question. I turned on the answering machine. But it was no use—I still couldn't work. So I went out, heavy with bandages, leaden with the care of Dr. Goldsmith.

The struggle within me was symbolic. Not good versus evil, but reason versus a reckless impulse to hail a taxi and ride to the Times building. "Guess what?" I would say. "Do you know who I am? I am the author of a significant work, a work of very great genius."

Was that *Eine Leerstelle* in the window of the Dalton bookstore?

Still in print. And the essays? *Permissible Loveplay*. Here they were, the collected works of Quayle, specially bound in a boxed set, the whole kit and caboodle.

I hurried down the street, protecting my arm in Napoleonic fashion and mumbling profane words.

"Yoo hoo!" someone called.

I turned, uncertain as to whether I was being hailed. It was someone across the street, an old woman waving, suitably dressed for Fifty-seventh and Fifth. I ducked into a department store, where I waited twenty minutes, moving along the aisles, purchasing two lipsticks and a scarf, anxious that I might be thought a shoplifter, the larceny in my heart unfurled.

I left the store. "Don't evade," my mother said. I would go home, confront the children. Passing a newsstand, I stopped to read an announcement. The *Village Voice* was conducting a colloquium, "Exploring the Universe of *Eine Leerstelle.*"

But where had I been while all this was happening? I had been in my place. I had been in my woman's place. Had I ever listened to Rosemary? Had I ever gone with her to one of those group sessions? "A swell bunch of women," Rosemary had said. "They lay it on the line, May. The real thing."

I decided to avoid public transportation. I felt too uneasy for the stops and starts. I began to jog. It was all right, I was wearing sneakers. I jogged, holding my arm stiffly against my chest, my breath coming in stertorous gasps.

I arrived home in a state of extreme disarray. They were

home before me. So I did mother's tasks. I ordered Richard to pick up his coat from the floor and hang it up neatly before I broke both his legs. I told Joanne that she did not have permission to accompany two of her friends for a glorious weekend in Peekskill. Joanne's reply: Do you think that I have to go away to do it? Is that what you think?

To do *it*?

Leon was pressing leaves into his scrapbook. He had stolen a branch of something autumn from a florist.

I forced myself into the rhythms of routine. I poured a glass of white wine, low in calories. I started dinner. I took out a casserole to defrost.

Joanne called reluctantly from her room, "Do you need any help? How's the arm?"

I called back: "No help! Fine arm!"

I was cutting up a salad when the doorbell rang. Harry no longer had a key that worked. I'd learned the first time around.

"Hi, old girl," he said. He was wearing grey flannel slacks and a tweed jacket. He looked prosperous. Maybe he even was.

"You didn't call," I said. "The rule is that you are to call. You are not just to appear."

I had made up all the rules. Not one of them was ever observed.

"In the neighborhood," he said. "Thought I'd see the kids." He caught sight of the arm. "What the hell happened?"

"Stabbed," I said. "Mugged."

"Here?" he said. "Here?" He tried to put his arm around me, but I was holding a bowl.

"No," I said. "There. Out there, somewhere."

"You shouldn't be alone," he said.

"The children. I am not alone."

"I'll stay for dinner," Harry said. "I'll help you. I brought ice cream."

44

There was an abrupt silence in the rooms. They were listening. "All right," I said.

Harry handed me the bag with the ice cream, and went to talk to Richard about football. He would reappear when dinner was ready. He would draw back my chair for me and wait with courtesy. "It's all your fault," Grace always said.

How had I ever found the courage to divorce the shit? I'd been so used to him. Harry could be so gentle. He was handsome. No one thought that I should divorce Harry. Three children, they said. Who will want you? At this age, is there romance? You've already had two chances. Allow him to repent. But I couldn't. Hadn't he come to my bed directly from another's? Wasn't his smile false? How many women had he had, the dirty crumb?

Little by little he became less real to me despite resemblances between him and the children. As for their characters, however, there was no resemblance. I preferred to believe they even despised him.

I set the table. I might have done it in the dining room—with five we would be crowded in the kitchen—but I chose not to make it an occasion. The plates, the silverware.

Joanne came into the kitchen. "He thinks Peekskill is okay."

"Then he can go," I said. I felt rancor. I felt rage. I would abandon them and flee the city.

"I'm just saying what he said," Joanne said and went back into the living room.

They had turned the television on. Loud enough for me to hear. We always listened to the news. My mother's doing. "The world," she said. "Pay attention."

The casserole was a lamb stew with carrots and potatoes and peas, the gravy was brown and bubbling. I had learned to cook when I was a girl. Good meals were favored, strong spicing, aromas. The revolution was well fed.

45

I paused, pepper still cascading into the casserole. What had I heard? Quayle? Now I was hearing *Quayle?* I went into the hall to look at the television screen. "Highlights of the coming week," say a TV voice. "Dick Cavett talks to Quayle—the man behind the book." And then there's that profile flashed—into how many decent American homes?

I felt sick. I had invented a mannikin, I had given it substance, I had stuffed straw into a fraudulence's suit. What would he say? What could he say? Could he even speak? Listen, he would have to speak of *Eine Leerstelle.* Was there time to write him a speech? Did he have one already?

"The creation of this work," he might say, "was accomplished in my small study. There in the presence of the artifacts of my life—various pieces of stone, various edges of brass, the Möbius strip of my intellect. The lighting was dim, the room was a cave, my mind was the world."

I went back to the kitchen, thinking to myself how my own profile would play in Des Moines. *Dick Cavett talks with May!*

I tried to remember what I'd been wearing back in the time of Quayle. Wasn't it a grey sweatshirt? The days had been cold, the apartment without heat. Yes, I must have worn a sweatshirt. My old coffee mug with *Mother* on it. The shade up because there was never any furniture to fade. Outside the window, Riverside Drive. A stretch of something like a park with old people in it, dogs, mothers of future generations. Poisoned treetops, beyond foul water where Quayle could go drown himself because he didn't deserve to live in the first place!

I took my hot-pads and reached for the casserole, and then I changed my mind. "Joanne!" I called. "Come carry this to the table. Dinner!"

They came to the table laughing. The boys were pushing Harry, and he pretended to be vanquished. Harry could be endearing. I decided to forgo a series of sayings,

46

like "Wash your hands!" or "Turn out the lights behind you because I pay the bills."

Harry pulled out my chair. "Here," he said. "Take it easy, old girl."

The illusion that we were a family persisted through dinner. Harry ceremoniously served the ice cream. It was chocolate, a dimensionless flavor.

"I had an offer," Harry began as I poured the coffee, "from a firm in Colorado. Denver suburb."

"You mean a job?" Joanne said. "All the way in Colorado?"

"Could we go?" Richard said, and looked at me.

"I'm going with Joanne," Leon said.

"An offer?" I said.

"A firm into computers," Harry said.

"What do you know about computers?"

"Selling, selling," he said. "They want me to go out for an interview."

"Go," Joanne said. "We could visit you. I could ski. I'd love to ski."

"If you are all finished," I said, "homework."

They stared at me.

"Move."

Harry helped me clear the table. He even put some plates in the dishwasher. I had to take them out and rinse them.

"Are you seeing a good doctor?" he said. "Can't fool around with your health, old girl."

"Yes," I said. "He's in the building."

Harry straightened up. "Baby," he said, "in order to go to Colorado for this interview, well, I'm a little short for the ticket and the hotel."

"Charge it."

"I would," he said, "but the account is temporarily shut down. I didn't make a payment on time. You know me and dates."

"I understand you had a few lately."

47

"What?" he said.

"How much?" I said.

"Five hundred."

I was going to scream. But the phone rang first. I was certain that it was ringing with abnormal volume. Joanne ran to get it. There was a phone in the hall and an extension in my alcove.

"For you!" she called.

The timing was good, my juices were flowing. Still, it might be anyone. It could be Grace. Another client. Anyone.

"I'll finish in here," Harry said. "I'll sweep the floor."

I may had nodded. I went into my alcove, closed the door, picked up the phone. I yelled, "Hang up, Joanne!" The hall phone clicked.

"Hello," I said. "This is May Alto."

"Mrs. Alto," the man said.

I felt a fresh, unknown thirst. The voice unheard for many years roared with familiar arrogance. He sliced each syllable. My Quayle had come to life. Listening was glorious—and real.

"Mrs. Alto?"

I could have socked the swine in the balls.

"Dr. Quayle," I said, "congratulations. Heartiest congratulations and felicitations on your extraordinary honor. I was surprised to hear about it, to read about it. Surprised and hugely delighted. Again, my congratulations."

My mind swam with images. My forefinger was drawing circles on my bandage.

"You called to congratulate me," Quayle said. He was careful with his emphasis—it was not a question.

"In part," I said. "In part."

"In part?"

"Yes," I said, "in part. Some of the part is to congratulate you. The rest of the part is to tell you I won't let it happen."

"Won't let it happen? I certainly don't understand. You

48

did some research for me once, Mrs. Alto, and I have done you the courtesy of returning your call."

I admired, I admired the cool little speech, the conversation tone, the total lack of trembling. Not one snippet of concern exposed. Yet there he was on the telephone.

"You are not home-free," I said. "With the prize. I will not let it happen."

"I don't understand. I do not understand. Mrs. Alto, I will now hang up. I will now terminate this call."

"No," I said. "You will pay."

"Absolutely do not comprehend, and I must go."

"Newspapers," I said. "The press. The media."

"What?"

"I'll talk."

"But who would believe you?" he said. Oh, the confident, respectable, unscrupulous bastard.

"Proof," I said.

"No proof, Mrs. Alto. Old notes, drafts of *my* books, are not proof. I will deny this, I will make you regret."

"In the book," I said. In my book, a book written by me, a book written by a woman in the prime of her life, "are tales of mine."

"Do not prolong this," Quayle said. "I have calls to make."

"My mother. In your book," I said.

"Your what?"

"My mother. Pages one hundred twenty-nine through one hundred forty of the first *authorized* edition."

"Impossible."

"How would you know? You barely read those drafts." I was suddenly annoyed. So many clients scarcely read their material. All that work and effort unappreciated.

I heard paper. He was turning pages. He was looking for the passages. That's how well he knew his book.

"And my aunt," I said.

"Your aunt?"

"Giselle. Now I want—"

"Be still," he said. "Say no more on this phone. I will call you tomorrow."

"I will wait," I said.

"Not in your apartment. Go to the Plaza Hotel at one o'clock. I'll have you paged for a call. At that time give me the phone number of a telephone booth on a street corner."

"Hey," I said, "no one is listening."

The phone clicked.

How odd that at the conclusion of that call it was I who felt like the victim. I had the impression that I was about to crumple or disappear. The room seemed very silent, as if the world was listening to my walls.

Was Quayle at this moment turning to his wife, that lady in the yellow hat, and weeping? Did he cry, "Doom, doom"? Did his wife comfort him? My mother believed in anarchy, power to the people, no government, communal life. She had conviction. I had convictions. Quayle had none. I felt better at once. It was true—what did Quayle believe in?—whereas look at me.

I went back to the kitchen. Harry had swept the floor, had put everything away. The dishwasher hummed. Was the jacket that he wore new? I didn't recognize it.

"Listen," he said, "maybe you can spare a couple of hundred."

I shook my head. "No," I said, "I'll lend you the entire five hundred."

Harry looked surprised. He scratched the side of his head. "All of it?"

"All of it."

My ship was arriving, pulling into a Swedish port. I wrote Harry a check. He folded it and carefully placed it inside what looked to be a brand-new wallet.

"Could I hang around?" he asked. "Spend the evening even if you're working? Watch TV?"

"I'll just work for a little while," I said.

I went to my alcove and pulled out the Quayle folder. It was old but intact. There were all the index cards with my notes. My outline for the first draft. A wonderful sheet of paper on which Quayle had written "I like this. Q."

By the following day I had to have a thorough plan in hand. How much to ask for? I had decided. The entire prize. Yes, I'd take the whole sum. It was mine.

But the prize money wasn't enough. Who could consider it enough? Wasn't the fame also mine?

A monthly retainer! Like an old family servant put to pasture. Like a food-giver. A fair exchange in return for all that meat and drink.

The prize money *and* a monthly retainer.

Before we spoke again, I would have to know exactly how much Quayle was worth. I would be fair.

I still had the original copy of Quayle's resume. His life history on one page. I pulled down the most recent edition of *Who's Who*. I found Quayle's entry. It had fattened, all right. Honors, clubs, societies. Some past! *Eine Leerstelle* and *Permissible Loveplay*. His life's work. After the *m.* was the name of the lady of the yellow hat. Two children.

Distinguished life. Certainly was a distinguished life. I laughed, I roared, I guffawed. It made my arm ache. Harry opened the door.

"What's up?"

"Nothing," I said. "Something just occurred to me. Client matter."

Harry closed the door.

Quayle had changed his schools. I giggled as I carefully compared my sheet of paper with the entry.

Different schools.

Six

The derivation of my vengeance was the Old French word *maille* that means small coin or the German word *Mahl* that means tribute. There was also a Gaelic word *mal* that means rent, but I don't think that was what I thought about. The *black* referred to the base metal—usually copper—that was used to pay these demands.

And, of course, everyone ended up in jail. Or was burned at the stake. Sometimes they were dragged off by a man in a grey fedora for a reading of the Federal Criminal Code (18 U.S.C. 873): "Whoever, under a threat of informing, or as a consideration for not informing against any violation of any law of the United States, demands or receives any money or other valuable thing"—is guilty of it.

I had decided to wear my best client outfit even for the telephone call. I knew what that was. That was the damned cloak of respectability. It was while I chose scarf and gloves that the phone rang. I picked up the receiver, not letting it touch my ear.

"How's your arm?" Grace asked.

My arm, I realized, burned. It looked as if a bicycle pump had gone to work under the gauze. No time for the doctor.

"I'm fine," I said. "Much better."

"Good," she said. "Do you want to have lunch? I'm taking the day off. I'm depressed."

"I can't," I said. "Not today. I have an appointment."

Grace sighed. "Can't you break it, postpone it? I had a terrible evening. I went out with a monster. Only you would appreciate what I've been through."

"Sorry," I said. I checked my watch. I had some financial matters to estimate. "Must go."

I left the Midtown Library at noon. I planned to arrive at

the Plaza early. I wanted my voice to sound very calm. I would meditate on calmness. My new notes were in a black leather briefcase.

I was still slightly amazed. Who would have suspected? Quayle was rich, trusted, loaded. I had never considered his wife's maiden name before. Virginia family, old money, pots and pots of well-aged money.

I might take the children on a skiing trip to Colorado—rent a chalet. We could do things. I tried to keep my thoughts in check as I walked up Fifth Avenue. I was wearing a dark grey suit and a white blouse with a bow at the neck. I was dressed for success.

Nevertheless, despite my new knowledge, I was going to be sensible. Not too much. I thought of the perils of blackmail. But wasn't this situation different? This was no personal darkness that was being concealed here. Quayle could not turn to his wife and say, "This girl." This girl, he couldn't say. A moment's passion, he couldn't say. So I wasn't faced with his possible escape from an escapade, an indiscretion, a touch of madness. It meant nothing—he couldn't say that, either.

Would his wife have ordered him out?

What I was blackmailing Quayle for was his life. His life belonged to me.

Quayle was my greatest creation.

Yes, I thought about coming clean. About publicly announcing the truth. The work was mine and only mine. And what would happen? The honor removed, the story a scandal.

And *Eine Leerstelle*? The essays—*Permissible Love-play*? They would certainly be discredited. Not read, not studied. My mother and Aunt Giselle abandoned; Trasker too. Had I ever intended oblivion for that work? I was proud of it! I respected it!

At three past one I was paged in the lobby. "Mrs. M. Alto," the voice called. It was Quayle. Of course. "The

53

number," he said in a muffled voice.

I gave him the number. "It will take me five minutes to walk to that booth from here," I said.

"Write down my number," he said.

"Your number?"

"Certainly. From your booth you will call me. Have plenty of change, it's long distance."

"Hell," I said, "let's talk now. It's cold outside."

He had already hung up.

I checked my change. There was a lot. Where was he calling from? Later, I would check the area code.

It was really cold outside, and a wind blew bits of paper everywhere. The arm hurt. Possibly a fever. I found the booth. So why wasn't it occupied the way it would be if this were Hitchcock?

The phone rang. I answered.

"I wanted to be certain you were calling from a street-corner booth," Quayle said. "Found out from the telephone company. Now call me back."

Twice he'd hung up on me. Twice! I was not about to permit this to continue. This had to stop right now.

I made a small pile of change on the metal ledge. With the door closed the booth smelled of urine. I was taking up the space of a pervert. I thought of someone standing out there and waiting, not threatening, just waiting for the shelter that I had taken. I couldn't vacate the booth. Did the person know that?

I plunged the coins into the slot and dialed the number. The operator interrupted. More coins, more loss. Then somewhere the circuits clicked, the bell rang, once.

"Who is it?" he said.

"Dr. Quayle, who would it be? Where are you talking from? Your office?"

"Of course not. I'm in a telephone booth."

"Good," I said. "I hope it's a cold one." I'd done a treatise once on the effect of weather on human behavior. I hadn't been convinced at first—thought it was like

54

accounts of what happened to you when Jupiter crossed Saturn.

"I do not have much time," he said. "Now what is this shit, Mrs. Alto? Is this about extortion?"

Extortion? Yes, this was about extortion, about criminal intent, about getting my own back. Maybe it was even a stick-up.

"No," I said. "Regard it as a delayed statement of damages for my labors."

"I don't know who you think you're dealing with," he said. "I am recording this conversation."

"Record away," I said. "My work on your behalf has not been fully paid for. *Comprende?*"

"You were paid in full for your research notes."

"My research notes!" The man was mad—Mars touching Jupiter. Was he trying to pay me for the souls of my mother and my Aunt Giselle, for their thoughts, their world? My research notes were the entire manuscript of *Eine Leerstelle* and two hundred and fourteen pages of essays, three of them an explication of *Eine Leerstelle*.

I was aware of a certain confusion about *Eine Leerstelle* within me. A dual nature. I now yearned for that book, it fulfilled me, and I remembered all of it. I had paced the room, as was customary when I was alone, and could shout out lines. Every word belonged to me. At the significant moment my mother had appeared and later, of course, Aunt Giselle, not to mention "Uncle" Trasker.

I could hear breathing.

"Stand fast," my mother had said, advice given to the tremulous when the press in the cellar was being smashed.

"May Alto," Quayle said, "I cannot believe this. We had a contract."

"No contract," I said. "No paper."

"A contract of honor," he said. "An agreement, an understanding. Clasped hands. Have you no ethical code?"

"*My* book," I said.

"*Mine*," he said.

I pictured the shit hunched over, his collar turned up as he bent to the receiver. The jerk perhaps even screening his mouth against lip-readers lingering nearby.

"Money," I said. "That's it, Quayle. That's the message—money."

"Never," said he.

At this metaphorical moment my life did not flash before my eyes nor did I want more than justice. Yet behind my back the glass door rattled, causing a severe disturbance in the region of my spleen.

"Hey!" the man outside the booth called, punctuating his words with more rattles. "What are you doing tying up the phone all day? You don't own New York, you know."

That man had a warm coat on, a big brown envelope under his arm. Didn't he have an office and a phone to go to? I waved him away. My arm went out in an expansive gesture, hit the pyramid of coins. They fled to the corners of the booth, sank into filthy patches of mold, fungi, bacteria galore. I wasn't going to pick up that crap. Touch the evil they'd touched?

Any moment now the operator would cut in. I wedged the receiver between cheek and raised shoulder as I maneuvered purse. More coins. Did I have any?

I was slow. The ruined arm would not do as it was told. My fingers, grown numb and bloated, received no messages as they flipped past tissues, notebook, pens. No more coins.

"I'm out of change," I said. "You will have to call back."

"Forget this nonsense," he ordered.

I shook my head, a poetic gesture. "Are you kidding? Forget? Forget what? I want. I'll get."

"Woman," he said, "this is impossible. I will not let you do this."

"Money," I said. "Money is the only answer."

His voice became softer. Had he spied an eavesdropper? "I have an appointment," he said. "I am late."

56

I believed him. I saw him push back his sleeve to look at his watch. Not digital, real hands, real numbers.

"I am not unreasonable," I said. "Call me back tonight, and I will state my terms. Or do I call the New York *Times*?"

"This booth at seven," he said.

I tried to feel my forehead, but the hand was icy, the reading not accurate. This booth at seven? The question was who was in charge. Should the blackmailee be permitted to dictate to the blackmailer? Besides, when the sun went down, this booth would be a meat locker, and I would be subject to weird behavioral changes.

"Seven's okay," I said. "But at my place, got it?"

"The booth," he said.

"My place."

"You are planning something. What are you planning, May Alto?"

"Nothing more than I have told you—the cost of my silence."

"I will not call you at home," he said.

"You will," I said and hung up.

It was pleasant to think of him standing there with the receiver uselessly in hand.

How I got home who knows, but the point is I did. One minute I was outside the booth and the next I was unlocking my door. I must have walked. I must have passed people. Didn't I see a man in pursuit of a boy—a boy about nine in a grey sweater ravelling at the elbows. Didn't I see that? The man shouting, "Just you wait!" He had a pole in his hands, maybe a broom handle.

Dropping coat and purse on the couch, I went into the kitchen and forced open the plastic lid of the aspirin bottle kept by the sink. Three aspirins would work marvels. It was essential that I deceive the body's temperature back to normal. I could not afford another moment of daze. I could not afford any mistakes—arm or no arm. The bandage felt tight, so I sliced it off with a kitchen knife.

And that arm—no longer my arm—that arm was a thin-skinned tropical fruit, emerging pale pink from the shoulder, a deeper color you did not want to look at as it ripened farther down and became globular—ending somewhere hideous in a shade I think they call magenta. A tracery of purple fruit veins spread out from the core.

I would heal that arm by following Trasker's counsel, given literally in *The Power of Positive Thinking*. I would sit quietly, unmoving in my chair. The body at rest, calling up its resources. I took my three aspirins, swallowed with water. Had I swallowed the three aspirins?

I poured a cup of cold coffee. Everything was done with one hand. It was possible, I could manage. I went into my alcove, my fiefdom, and sat down to consider the question of Quayle.

Shouldn't I consider the question of Quayle? Shouldn't I consider the question of Quayle considering me? Quayle pacing the floor, Quayle searching his papers for clues, Quayle looking for written evidence. Something he should burn? Hey, Quayle, does May Alto stalk you down corridors in your sleep? Does she have a face? The same face she had when she sat across from you? You turned the pages, you fake, a speed-reader. "Sounds all right to me," you said.

"That's what I thought," I said.

"And the title?" you said.

"*Eine Leerstelle*."

"Um," you said, and turned a bit to the right. "I like that. Yes, I like that."

I took an index card and made a note. I would have to do a literature search for articles that dealt with *Eine Leerstelle*. How well had my meaning been deciphered? Did they get it?

I should concentrate on the telephone call. I must plan, rehearse. My money, I must say. My words, I must say. No hesitation, no betrayal of weakness, no fidgeting. Quayle would leap, pounce, eviscerate. Quayle, I would

58

say. Quayle, I want such-and-such. I must be specific, give terms—state them.

My mother sat in the room.

Also, Aunt Giselle.

They were dressed in black. My mother in a black pants suit with a cotton blouse buttoned high at the neck, and Aunt Giselle in a black crepe dress trimmed in lace. They were in mourning. Their clothes smelling of mothballs. I could think of several funerals they might have attended. Someone had cut my mother's hair, and it was too short in the front. Aunt Giselle looked all right, frail and distant. Yes, they were in mourning, although they would neither wail nor cry. It had to be from a section in a book. But which book? Could it have been in *Eine Leerstelle*? Was it in *Death Comes for the Archbishop, Death in Venice, Death Is a Little Man, Death of a Hero, Death of a World, The Death of the Gods, The Death Ship*?

"Throw away nothing," my mother said.

"I won't," I said.

"Everything can be used."

"Yes," I said.

"Save emotions," Aunt Giselle said. "The mind and heart together."

"Do you have anything to drink?" Mother asked.

"Help yourself," I said.

I could use some advice. "First things first," I said. "What shall I ask for?"

"Everything," Mother said. "Take the bastard! Rob the robber! Take everything he's got."

"Heart," Aunt Giselle said.

"I've been thinking," I said. "The prize money. Of course, the prize money."

"Wise," Mother said. "But more."

"A retainer," I said. "Maybe three hundred a month."

"Five," Mother said. "Remember my philosophy."

"Jesus," Joanne said. She was afraid to touch the arm or

59

the hand. I knew this although I was uncertain whether I was still sitting in the chair or was now standing against the wall across the room.

"She looks terrible," my daughter said.

"What'll we do?" Richard said.

"I'm scared," Leon said.

I heard all of this, and I opened my eyes, or my eyes were already open. "Hey," I said. "Are you home from school already? I must have been napping."

"Red like a beet," Joanne said. "Don't you know that?" Her fingers straight from Perry's expedition glazed my forehead. "You got to have a zillion fever."

The aspirins? What had happened to modern science? "Get me some aspirins," I said. "I'll be fine. I'll make dinner. What would you like?"

"Hamburgers," Richard said.

"Shut up, stupid," Joanne said. She looked at me. "You can't make any dinner. You got to have a doctor."

"Should I call Dad?" Richard said.

I wanted to protest. But I was busy with my warm glow. I liked that warm glow.

"No," Joanne said, her tone bossy. "Leon, you go to the hall closet and pull out the little suitcase."

"Me?" Richard said.

"You stay here with Mom while I call."

"Call?" I said. "Call whom?" Not Quayle, I hoped. Besides, shouldn't the line be free?

"Grace," Joanne said. "I'll call Grace."

Did Grace still like me? It was Grace who had lent me lipstick. He'll never look at you pale that way. Be bright, be red. She gave me lipstick to entice Benjamin. Grace and I had been friends, and we had gone to rallies together. Unless that wasn't Grace.

The sound was a doorbell. Our doorbell was not a true doorbell. It was a buzzer. The buzzer sounded once, twice, three times. I knew that Joanne was there and that Leon and Richard were standing back.

60

"Where is she?" Rosemary asked.

It was Rosemary, then, and not Grace.

"In her alcove," Joanne said. "She really looks awful."

"Don't worry, kiddo," Rosemary said. "We'll fix her up. We better hurry. Grace is downstairs in a No Parking."

"Richard," Joanne said. Her voice snapped the word. "Carry the suitcase down to the car. Leon, you stay up here. One sniffle and I'll split your skull."

They helped me stand up. Joanne held the good arm, and Rosemary had her hands on my waist pulling upward.

"Unnecessary," I said.

There was the elevator, the car. "My God!" Grace said.

I rode in the car, my head on Rosemary's shoulder. Already I felt better. The doctor would give me a shot, then I would go home. Wasn't money at stake? Money was at stake.

"I think that you will be with us for a while," the doctor said.

It was cold in the hospital, drafts in the hall. Nothing like external chill. White is a cold color anyway.

"No," I said.

"Absolutely," Rosemary said. "I'm going to Admitting." She had my Blue Cross card. "I found it in your wallet," she said.

"What time is it?"

"Eight o'clock."

"Eight." It was already too late. I might as well be sick. "All right," I said. "I'll spend the night."

"Ah," said the doctor. He was foreign, but his English was very good.

"What will you do?" I asked.

"Prevent dehydration," he said. "You've got lots of edema, pain, suppuration."

He would have said more, but they were taking me away on a rolling cot edged with chrome and a silvery hoar.

"Have to run," Rosemary called to my departing body.

"Grace is outside. Don't worry about the kids."

I remained, I though, conscious. There was a gentle irrigation of the wound. "Gram-positive or gram-negative?" I asked.

No one answered me.

Everyone was busy with prophylactic therapy.

I'm going to be rich, I wanted to say. Endogenous sources. Hadn't I heard something about a synergistic infection?

"You're very courageous," someone said. "This must hurt."

"Thank you," I said. Let us prevent dehydration. "Tell me," I said, "is there an old lady in the Emergency Room? A little old lady with terrific legs?"

"She's delirious," someone said.

"That's why it doesn't hurt her," someone replied.

Of course it hurt me. Why wouldn't it hurt me, all that digging and rutting in my body. Maybe I should leave. How? Grace had driven Hers away. I didn't have my car—Harry did. Could I call Benjamin? Where the hell was Benjamin these days? Benjamin had a blue convertible. I have never before or since known a man with a blue convertible. You can understand the attraction. It was the palest birth of Prussian blue. Benjamin's interest in me had a lot to do with his belief in the innocence of the young. Anyway, liking me was daring. She's dangerous, his friends said. The whole family.

My mother didn't think much of Benjamin. "Politically backward," she said. "I'm thinking," she said, "about the son of our cousins in Minneapolis. The commingling of revolutionary blood. He would be the perfect choice. I fought side by side with his parents."

I anticipated a battle—a Parthian battle—my expectations weren't good. I considered fleeing. Grace gave me a lipstick. "Be attractive," she advised. "Lower your neckline. Be seductive." Grace loaned me a dress, a scarf. Mother wrote to Minneapolis.

*

My arm floated upward. It sailed around and around, never touching the walls. It glowed with a phosphorescent certainty. It was a big red kite, silky and smooth. So Leon had finally gotten the goddamn thing airborne.

I tried a breathing exercise—counting my gasps. Ah one, ah two. I made herculean efforts to recall how this had happened. Was the damage irreversible? I became a mourner for myself. I sought comfort in self-hypnotism. I, May Alto, I whispered. I raised myself on one elbow and stared at the bottle of saline.

I turned on the pillow. There was a cord, a lime-green cord. I pulled the cord and a plastic bulb covered with buttons landed on the bed. You could do a lot with those buttons. The soft and loud of sounds, the bringing of the nurse, the lights, the up and down of existence. I pushed for the light. Darkness outside.

Already I felt delirium was slipping away, the plague of foggy thoughts. Forgetting came fast, I knew. I pushed for the nurse.

No nurse appeared. There was a voice instead from a lime-green box on the wall. "May I help you?" said the voice.

"Paper," I begged. "Paper, any kind, a pad, a few sheets. A pencil. A pen."

"In the morning," the voice said.

"Now!"

"Would you like something to help you sleep?"

I'd lost, been defeated. The paper would not come in time.

No paper, no pencil. Not even a thirty-nine-dollar recorder. How I would have loved to have later knowledge of my exact thoughts, reactions. How useful for future work. I tried to create a suitable acronym for my feelings, the colors, the occasional bird of darkness that tried to peck its way through the glass window, the spectres of kin, the unsuitable apparitions. But they were departing as I tried to define them. I numbered some images. I had sixty-seven distinct and discrete visions.

Had I been this sick before? Who remembered? I equated illness with stress, with improper care, with sin, with guilt.

Forget it. I refused to consider guilt. Drop guilt! Too late to backtrack now. Me versus Quayle. How did he see me? As sponge rubber. And himself? As steel.

I found my watch on the bedside table. It was nine o'clock in the morning. What I wouldn't give for one sheet of paper. I should be recording those sixty-seven illusions, some with a tart odor. Also, the twelve colors that shuddered past the bed, waves and beacons.

By three o'clock I was alone in the room. I knew that. The room was in the hospital. I identified all the furniture. The bed next to mine was empty. The darkness beyond the window grew less opaque. One glowing star turned out to be only the light from a distant window. Where, I decided, a woman sat alone at a table and wept.

At five o'clock the arm was pink, the fingers bent without difficulty. I didn't like the intravenous bottle, the plastic tubing, the needle that neatly pinned me to immobility. I realized that I had been sweating and that I was no longer warm.

I was me again. The previous evening had happened—Rosemary, Grace, the children. Gone were my visions.

But the advice from some of the apparitions was good. After all, I came from practical stock—so I'd up the ante to five hundred on the retainer bit. Like Mother said, "All people are worthy. But take care of your rear."

The window flamed with sunlight. I was all right. I was ready for action.

Quayle, I'm coming.

I pushed for the nurse.

"May I help you?" said the box.

"I want to leave," I said. "Be discharged."

"Doctors come at eight."

"Now!"

"Doctors come at eight."

64

"My children," I said, allowing a gasp in my voice. "My children are alone. Three children alone."

"Doctors come at eight."

So I had time to consider the situation.

Quayle calling last night. Quayle ringing, no May to hear it. What must he have thought? I contemplated his lurching, his bristling, his heaving. Anger at first. Your Quayle was not to be kept waiting. No one kept your Quayle waiting! Not the lady in the yellow cloche. Not the people sitting outside his door. Anger, was he ever angry! Reddened face, blood vessels maddened in dilation? No, Quayle takes a drink, one neat Scotch. How dare she? he thinks, he bubbles, he screeches.

What then? I looked at the bottle dripping away into my arm. Fear, that's what. Your Quayle afraid. Your Quayle checking the radio. Does he think that it will be a news bulletin? Nobel Prize winner exposed! But hearing no word was more fearsome than knowing. He twirls the radio knob—stations fade in and out. Snatches of late-night sound, country music, desperate souls.

Oh May, he weeps. May, where are you?

Here.

At eight, they came on rubber heels smelling of coffee. I made a scene, and was discharged. The doctor shook his head. "Against medical advice," he said.

"I accept that," I said.

They made me sign a paper. May Alto leaving against medical advice. I was giving up my legal claim to get back at them. I wasn't abandoned, though. They gave me medications, they wished me well.

Even a short stay in hospital did things to the world. I had lost my feeling of time. Time did not move fast for me. I was not surprised by icicles on the trees, snow choking the road. Short, stocky women shoveling. I was not surprised. It was my kind of time.

I stood on the sidewalk. All around me were people

going to work. I was going home. I waved my arms, I jumped up and down. I caught the attention of a taxi looking for a person. The air was sharp and cold and felt wonderful.

"They let you go?" Joanne said. "I didn't think they'd let you go so soon. Grace was going to see you this morning."

"I'm all right," I said. I held out my arms, benf them, straightened them. "See?"

"Well," Joanne said, "you look all right."

Leon and Richard looked pale, subdued. I stooped and kissed them. No one pulled away. They smelled of fresh soap, frightened into cleanliness by Joanne no doubt. "I'm fine," I said. "Sore arm. That's all."

"You'll be here for dinner?" Richard asked.

"Yes."

"Good."

"Grace took us to Burger King," Leon said.

"Yeah," Joanne said. "She's asleep on the couch."

"Through all the noise?" I couldn't believe it.

"She didn't want to sleep in your bed. Thought it might be catching."

"What did she do with her car?"

"Bribed the super across the street. He found a place in the garage between two Lincolns. Grace thought it'd be all right there."

Joanne hoisted her book bag. That was the signal. They were gone.

In the living room Grace slept on the couch, fearful of contagion. She didn't snore. I would have thought that she was the person to snore. Her shape beneath the quilt was small. She was larger when standing, bigger all over. The quilt was new, covered with green and white striped ticking. It was not attractive. Joanne must have given it to her. The emergency quilt from the hall closet. No linen from my bed with its hint of the plague.

66

Neat, tidy Grace had tossed her clothes on the chair. We weren't the girls of our youth anymore. Had we been friends? We had been the girls of our youth, that we couldn't undo, friends or whatever it was, and now she slept on my couch.

I went into the kitchen and made coffee. I rattled pots, slammed cupboard doors. I turned on the radio. I sang.

Grace woke up. "Hullo?" she called. "Joanne?"

I went back to the living room, stood in the doorway. "Me," I said.

"My God! What are you doing here? You shouldn't be here."

"I'm back from the hospital."

"They let you go? Don't tell me, May, they let you go?"

"They let me go."

"Irresponsible," Grace said. "I'll get dressed."

"Listen, Grace," I said. "I am grateful, you know, grateful for everything."

The boys. I had forgotten Grace's twins. "Your children?"

"Three days with their father," Grace said. "Bad influence."

"Anyway," I said, "thanks. You didn't have to spend the night, though. Joanne could have managed."

"That's what she said. But I say, May, how can you trust a sixteen-year-old girl? No way, I told her. Think of that next time. Remember, sixteen isn't that old. Think of us at sixteen."

"Yes," I said.

"I'll get up now," Grace said. "Get dressed."

"Clean towels on the shelf above the sink," I said.

I went back to the kitchen and looked at my watch. How long would she stay? Grace, forgive me my thoughts.

Grace, that speed demon, flew into her clothes, patted her face dry, and came into the kitchen. She was ready to go. But first she must sit at the table with me and sip her coffee, must retell the night's adventures—my rescue, the trip to the hospital, the bedding of the car.

I listened. I felt good. Grace pinned up slipping strands of hair, frowned, fixed her lipstick.

"I have a date tonight," Grace said. "He's new. Someone new."

"Wonderful," I said. "Have a marvelous time."

"Are you all right? Are you delirious?"

I touched my forehead. "Fever-free," I said. "It must be the power of morning. I feel within me the pulsing of existence. As if there is nothing that I cannot achieve. Yet why haven't I, Grace? Why haven't any of us? Should we have been more like our mothers?"

"You read too much," Grace said. "I always said that you read too much. Who wanted to be like our mothers? Did you? Me? Huldie? Rosemary?"

"No," I said, filled with honest fruit. "No. I wanted a mother like everyone else's. But styles change."

"Not," Grace said, "that my mother wasn't a fine woman. Weren't they all fine women? May they rest in peace. But all those meetings, May. All that humanity coming at us. I wanted to be a private person. Didn't you want to be a private person?"

That was it. That was it. I was unworthy because of what I had wanted. My mother wanted only noble things. I wanted patent leather shoes, I wanted blond curls, I wanted new dresses and a red coat with a fur collar. Didn't Grace have a red coat with a fur collar when she was a girl? Of course. And the shoes too.

"The time," Grace said. "My God, the time. I promised to drive Hers away by ten."

"Let me pay for the garage," I said.

Grace shook her head. "What are friends for? Anyway, it wasn't much."

I nodded, reluctant to block generous impulses.

"Oh," Grace said as she buttoned her coat. "I almost forgot. You have some nut pestering you."

"What?"

"The telephone," Grace said. "A man has been calling

you on your telephone. Has this happened before? You should have left the phone listed in Harry's name. It's women they're after."

I practiced control. I kept my voice calm. "Why a nut? What made him sound like a nut?"

"I didn't know it was a telephone pervert at first. He called early eveningish. Asked for you."

Quayle, my Quayle had not forsaken me.

"Then maybe it was someone I knew. Maybe it was."

"Then you better unknow him, that's all I've got to say. This guy called and asked for you. Not here, I said. Bang went the receiver. Called again at ten. Asked again. I recognized the voice. Bang. Called again at midnight. Didn't say a word, but of course it was him. At one o'clock I was asleep when the phone rang. I said enough of this. I took the receiver off the hook. Where did you meet him? Do you know him? Is he that poet?"

I shook my head. "No, not the poet. I don't know who this could be. Some nut."

"At least he isn't a breather. I had one two years ago—remember? The police said don't worry. What do they care? Anyway, these sex maniacs give up after a while. Just hang up if he calls again."

"Right."

"Well, I must go. Hers is waiting. But are you certain that you feel all right? The hospital can't be trusted. I could come back after I take my car home."

"No, no," I insisted. "I feel all right. I'll take it easy, take my medicine."

I closed the door, secured the dead-bolt. I whistled the Triumphal Procession from *Aïda*. Quayle had called. Quayle had called over and over. What a fine thought—Quayle in the waiting room of life.

Still, that wasn't the purpose. I mustn't allow the purpose to be diluted. I controlled my exhilaration. I took my medicine.

The question to be answered was whether I should call

Quayle. I hunted for the telephone that Grace had buried beneath pillows and replaced the receiver. Checked to see if it still worked. Lovely buzz sound.

Should I wait further? I was inexperienced in this matter. Uncertain as to the degree to which anxiety increased vulnerability. I went to get my shoebox of note cards to check again the Quayle entries. I would have to determine his actions from what I knew. From how many? From four meetings. Four times of actual contact, eye-to-eye, that was. Eight telephone conversations.

I walked back and forth, stalking game in my alcove. Conjuring up our Quayle as a boy. Quayle in a blue flannel blazer sitting in the classroom. Any classroom. A boy at ease, his hands loosely clasped. Pen in hand, the crud writes the answers in ink on his palms. What answers? Any answers. Even odds those hands don't sweat— those dry, smooth palms with microscopic words. No sniveling, cringing Quayle waiting to be caught. No loser early anointed. At the appropriate moment after use or at the sniff of danger, a juicy spit, and the slate wiped clean. Wiped clean by the white cotton handkerchief ironed by the day woman. Pen leaked, Quayle explains.

In truth, I was no seamless wonder of virtue. Didn't I cheat? A bit of paper, a list of dates insinuated up the sleeve of the sweater. Then the tremulous wait to be caught, cheeks flushed, mouth dry. Beginner's breasts heaving with fear. Nothing natural. "You," she said, one harridan or another from the past. Her fingers tapped the edge of the desk there by the canal meant to hold the pens, touched never-to-be-obliterated initials, my own included. School property not to be defaced. The hearts and words, the prehistory of graffiti. "You," she said. I was trapped, hanged, burned, defiled forever. "I should have expected it," she said. Everyone knew, everyone expected, everyone was one with her—united in despising. Wasn't I the only one with a mother so bad? A mother arrested.

But I meant to concentrate on Quayle, I meant to think only of Quayle. Did Quayle pull girls into the back seat of the family sedan? You bet. "Don't worry," he soothed, his hand running professionally up their silken sides. "Nothing will happen. I promise. Didn't I promise?"

Then came the tears, the shouts. "Can she prove anything?" Quayle's father asked.

"No," Quayle said. "She can't prove anything."

I wouldn't forget that the identity of Quayle's father was in question. One paper named him Charles Edward, but another said John Andrew.

What to do? Should I call Quayle now? Did extortionists have rules of etiquette? I looked out my window down at the park. I knew exactly what I saw, and it filled me with despair. A boy, no more than fourteen, being chased by a man carrying a piece of bamboo. The boy didn't have a sweater on, this time a grey vest. Another person sitting on a bench with a big brown envelope beneath his arm watched.

The phone rang, the sound shooting through the rooms. Good! Him first. Twice the bell sounded before I answered the call.

"Hello," I said.

"You," he hissed.

Quayle when last seen. The length of his fingers, ectomorph's fingers. The three-quarter profile with the portrait lighting coming from beneath each rosewood shelf. Quayle wearing a fine tweed jacket woven in an ancient Druid pattern.

I was there.

"I'll say goodbye to you then," he said.

I must have worn my raincoat.

"Yes," I said. "Goodbye."

I folded the check.

"How dare you!" Quayle said. "How dare you! Where were you last night? What were you doing?"

"Sorry," I said. "Unavoidable."

"What filthy plan are you plotting, May Alto? What are you up to?"

I marveled at his lack of self-control, but I didn't expect too much from it. I had constantly to reevaluate Quayle. Of course, it would have been easier if I had known about his background.

"The big kill," I said. "Pay-up time."

"You were paid," Quayle said, his cool once again in place.

"Hardly," I said. "You paid me for the manuscript. Now you must pay me for the prize."

"The prize is not being given to you."

"It should be."

That was true. Yet I could not see myself there—maybe embracing the King of Sweden. That's how much I thought of myself.

"I have already considered rejecting the prize."

"You expect me to believe that," I said. "On what grounds?"

"I could do it," he said. "A gesture, a fine gesture by the author of *Eine Leerstelle*. Unsuitable for the author of *Eine Leerstelle*."

That caught me for a moment. That took me by surprise. Could he have understood? Could he have grasped the meaning? No chance of that. It must have been suggested to him.

"That doesn't matter," I said. "Accept the prize or give it up—nothing changes. It would still have been offered to you."

The pause. I felt how much he wanted it, flecks of foam appearing at the corners of his mouth. He would never give up that prize. No way, not my Quayle.

"You could be incarcerated," he whispered.

"Say 'Go to jail,' " I insisted.

"Jail!"

"Scandal," I said. "Basically, a long-term scandal.

After the initial excitement come the analyses, the theses, the articles on ethics. You might even become a proper noun—*quayling*."

"What do you want, woman?"

"What I want," I said. "I want the prize money. Not a part of it, not a quarter of it, not a half—the whole of it. And that's just for starters, sweetheart. Next comes the monthly stipend, the retainer, the ever-blooming honorarium. Five hundred a month."

"Never."

"Yes."

"Impossible."

"I give you one week," I said. "I want half the money then."

"Two weeks."

"Agreed."

"*Wahooee!*" I yelled. "*Wahooee,eee.*" Round and round the room I marched with a baton twirler's high step. No one to see, no one to watch. I got you, you bastard. I was getting my own back. I was upsetting that apple cart. Never you mind the consequences.

Yes, good sense had deserted me. Scream, scream, scream. *Quayle! Quayle! Quayle!* May your mouth fall open in pain and fear and saliva drool out, ruining all tweeds forever. Goodbye, May, you said. Done with you, you thought. Passed from existence, synapsed away. Paid in full.

Done with me. Not ever, my new friend. Not ever. *Wahooee.* I will be king—no, no. I will be queen.

I tumbled on the rug, did a back flip, pants legs slipped to my calves.

I would say to the children—Ask me for something. Ask me for anything. I will buy it. Nay, *Quayle* will buy it.

"*Yahoo.*" I threw the cushions off the couch. One landed on end, a velvet puff. I kicked it. I had won.

Eine Leerstelle would live, survive, exist. After all of us were gone, it would be here.

It was then that exhilaration left me, then that I sat on the floor, head in hands. The opposite of guilt being innocence. Confession was a symbol. Confession performed for the sake of peace. Absolution from the Latin *absolutio*.

Seven

If you circulate in the vicinity of crime, suffer its climate, you eventually reach blame. From the Greek which we understand to mean evil speech. So there I was in circulation. Was I a Master Criminal?

I turned to routine. Routine was good, routine was always there. Rise at seven, feed the children, wash. Examine the weather. There was, I believed, no trace of paranoia in my view of the world. All was approached with open curiosity. I let my motives alone—figuring if I did, they'd do the same for me.

Leon came into the kitchen. "What are you making?" he asked.

"*Zuppa di pesce*," I said.

"Yum," he said. "Listen, I got a problem."

I put down my spoon and turned around. "What?"

"Mathematics."

"Arithmetic."

"Arithmetic. Can you help me?"

"I'll try. Read it to me while I stir."

He went to get the book. It had a glossy red cover. *New Numbers*.

"This one," he said. "*If Giselle bought thirteen apples from the fruit seller Sonya and gave three of them to*

74

Trasker and ate one and returned four wormy ones to Sonya, how many would she have left?"

I wiped my hands. "Get a pencil," I said.

My arm was not healing—three times a day I examined it. Once I thought I felt tiny, hard particles beneath the skin.

"Shrapnel?" Dr. Goldsmith said unkindly. "From a knife wound?"

So I threw away Dr. Goldsmith's pills and switched to a variety of remedies, cool water washes, proprietaries well-recommended, colored tinctures, poultices of tea leaves.

"Go to another doctor," Joanne said.

"Later," I said.

The UPS man brought a package with books— copies of Mrs. H.'s book.

Some clients I could do without. Not speaking about Quayle, of course. Quayle actually wasn't a bad client as those people go. It wasn't that Quayle thought about the reader. I thought about the reader. And that's why *Eine Leerstelle* was such a hit—an all-time best seller. I consider the reader. The client is one thing, the reader is another. Take Mrs. H. now, a rich client—a pain in the ass. Compared to her, my Quayle was a sweetheart.

Mrs. H. wanted the Caribbean, three affairs, three short pieces. She paid me in cash stuffed into an old Con Edison envelope.

Not the Caribbean again, I said. Would Mrs. H. listen? This is what I mean by lack of sympathy for the reader. I had done the Caribbean before—Jamaica, Spanish Town, the crazed lady. That *cri de coeur* when Trasker begs Rochester to leave the island.

The *official* published H. stories took place in 1912 in Austria. Giselle and the Correspondent, Giselle and the Archduke, Giselle and the Artist. The Artist painting Giselle in the nude. "He's no good," Sonya telling her. "Stick with the man with the power."

On Wednesday morning the sky was blue, and the

morning properly scheduled. People walked past me wrapped in colorful scarves and heavy woolen coats. I saw them, the children similar to mine, the babies wheeled by troubled mothers. I was thinking about that half-annoyed letter from my client Mr. L. I get maybe one letter a year like that. *I love everything except that description*, he wrote. *That description of my mother in the beginning. My mother was five feet nine, blond. In the book, it says short. Short, it says, stocky. With dark hair. Can that be changed?*

No, it can't.

I shopped at Gristede's, consulted my list, asked for delivery of the heavy bags, and bought a newspaper. Behind me I heard no echoing footsteps, did not glance sideways. There was, I noted, no bank robbery in progress at the corner, no citizen holding up another citizen with knife or club.

Still, there was someone around me. My mother had been often watched, also my aunts and uncles. But I–never. "Scavengers," my mother said. "Spies, takers of *trink gelt*, hands full of *vazyatha*."

I turned my head to the left. He was there all right. There in the doorway, there behind the stop sign. A man in a warm coat with a big brown envelope under his arm. His face was sallow, his eye hooded, a man who looked fifty, an old fifty. I reviewed in my mind the contents of my last will. I had named the guardians for my children. I had named Grace, Huldie, Rosemary.

Was I scared? Of course I was scared. I read the newspapers. During the previous year approximately sixty-five hundred assaults within a twelve-block radius of my apartment house. That is to say, twelve blocks in either direction. Sixty-five hundred assaults! Women objecting to the loss of property were pulled and dragged away. As for this one—no one would question this one. Ah, so he struck again, they'd say. So you should have known to watch out for that one, they'd say.

I pivoted once to look directly at the man. He was not

76

likable, he was well-nourished, his hands were chunky. In the cold air a drop of moisture hung stalactite fashion from his nose.

I carried nothing heavy in my purse, no weapon. If necessary I could scream. Then I decided to jog home. I would stick to the street, simulate speed, an athlete's strength, keep my neck arched. Suppose he grabbed me? How much pain could my arm bear? Still recovering from a mugging, the headlines would read. Mother of three. I thought about assailants, about assassinations, both political and otherwise.

Quayle had hired him.

That Quayle whom I did not know. The unknown Quayle who did not write *Eine Leerstelle*.

I jogged home, avoided the corner of the park. My shoes were wrong. My body fought the wind. It was an effort, but I remained alert and ready to scream.

I reached my building as three other women prepared to enter. I followed them inside, followed them to the elevator. "Yes," I said, "I am willing to join the Tenants' Association." We all nodded. I chatted willingly about deficiencies in the laundry room, about peeling paint, until the elevator reached my floor.

I ran down the hall to my apartment. Once inside, I locked and bolted the door. Neither my heartbeat nor my breathing would slow. It was coincidence, I thought. It must be coincidence. That man. Surely Quayle wouldn't risk everything this way. Would he?

Cautiously I went into my alcove and looked out the window. He was there in the park beneath my window. The cold was nothing to him in his warm coat as he sat on a bench eating an apple. He threw the core on the ground. This was surveillance.

I went at once to the telephone. To whom could I speak? Should I try 911? Could I tell Harry? Could I tell my friends?

This man, I would say, is after me.

Why?

Think, May—why is he after you?

Then I must say extortion, destruction, blackmail, threats, implied and actual.

I wanted to open the window and shout. "Go away! Hey, man, go away! You have been photographed, do you know that?"

I didn't have to pinch myself to face reality. I knew what could happen, what might happen. So I sat down at my table and wrote a brief account of the Matter of Quayle, indicating where the evidence could be found. The papers were folded and sealed in an envelope to be put into my safe deposit box. I labelled the envelope—*To Be Opened in Case of Death*.

But my powers of reasoning were nothing to sneeze at. Besides acquiring a man in the park, what else might Quayle do? Was Quayle thorough? Couldn't surveillance be insinuated into the home?

"Look over your shoulder," my mother had advised. "Take nothing for granted. When they're out to get you, they're out to get you."

I divided my rooms into squares and began the search like an explorer. There had been no repairmen in the apartment in recent weeks. Nothing new had suddenly appeared. What was I looking for? Tiny wires. Unexplained coils, strange bits of flaking plaster. This was not spring cleaning. I overlooked nothing—windows, doors. I removed the plates from outlets. I removed everything. I considered all possibilities. Futuristic gizmos that weren't even invented yet.

What did I find? A spoon, some coins, a cryptic note written by me that should be in the shoebox under "S."

Nothing, nothing, nothing. I sat on the floor, surrounded by the dry fruits of my excavation—snippets of this and that, melancholy drek.

My wrath began to grow. It built upward. Come after

me, would he! I thought of persecutors—Victor Emmanuel's speech in Rome. Mother and Giselle beside him on the platform urging him on. Quayle didn't stand a chance—it was in the blood. I would be relentless.

But anger led to irrational acts. When the bell went off, I got up, not even bothering to swat away the dust on my slacks. I flung open the door with abandon, never mind my careful training.

It was the man from the street, from the park, from the telephone booth. It was the man with his warm coat buttoned up to the neck and the big brown envelope beneath his arm.

My latest will lay unnotarized in the alcove. There was an upsurge in gastric activity. I pushed at the door with the arm that I could push with. Too late.

"May Alto," the man said, his foot jammed shrewdly between door and doorframe. "My card. I represent a person who would like to employ your services in the matter of writing. He wants you to prepare a book."

The man handed me his card. He handed me that big brown envelope. "Read the contents," he said. "My gentleman will call you." The man put a finger to his lips. "The key word," he said, "is *hush*."

This time he didn't kill me—next time that man might be representing someone else. I took the brown envelope to my alcove. What I had in my possession were four sheets of paper, three cheap, one high rag content with monogram. My new client was a businessman. *My name*, the client had written, *is a household word*.

Think, he wrote, *How for two hundred years my ancestors have influenced modern business--and—the world*.

He enclosed a list of important family contacts and a brief summary entitled "My Project." The book was to be privately printed.

I could start. It would keep me busy. I checked the calendar. There were still eight days to Quayle.

I made my notes as I read the project summary. I

prepared my cards for the file. Everything was ready when the phone rang. It was the new client.

"Ms. Alto," he said. "You have seen my needs. Can you relate to them?"

"Yes," I said. "I certainly can."

"Excellent," he said. "We will meet later. I will call."

I accepted the assignment, added ten percent to my fee. I was done with impractical thoughts, with self-reproach. I made a fresh pot of coffee and continued my notes.

The bank called. The manager's name was Perlod.

"Something of a problem here," Perlod said.

"What?" I said. "What?"

"Check number seven hundred thirty-four," Perlod said.

"My check number *seven hundred thirty-four*?"

"Yes," Perlod said. "This check issued to one Harry Alto. He says he is your husband."

"Was," I said.

"This Mr. Alto is here. The check seems to be changed, altered. The number says six hundred, but the written part shows signs of erasure. Looks like it might have been five. Our teller caught it. The check is being cashed right in your branch, you see. So we're verifying. Five or six?"

I wondered if Harry was sweating. If he stood casually at the manager's desk or slumped in a chair. His pose would be nonchalant. No, he wouldn't sweat, but his fingers would clench and unclench.

"Yes," I said. "The check was for six. Six hundred dollars."

Perlod was testy. "Then you should have rewritten the check. We really don't have to accept them this way."

"I'm sorry," I said. "It won't happen again."

"Very well. This once, then." Perlod did not believe me.

I hung up and sipped my coffee.

If you circulate in the vicinity of crime, you become in time a neighbor.

Eight

Think of the pressures. Why had I agreed to give him two weeks? Two days would have been more acceptable. Why did women always acquiesce? Two weeks, he had said. Certainly, I'd replied. Take two weeks.

I was stuck. Hell, I thought, I'll call him up. What was sacred about two weeks? Tomorrow is due-day, I'll say. But this I thought only at night. Mornings were different. In the early light of morning, uncluttered by a day's thoughts, I realized that my course was set. I could not let the power shift, my level of anxiety appear to exceed his. It had to be two weeks. After all, I had never tried extortion before. I was an amateur. How often did I do the biographies and memoirs of criminals? A few fugitive stories, the old chain gang, the odd hit-man for the big boys. No blackmailers, though—not a blackmailer in the bunch. Yet I was a quick study, wasn't I? Besides, the classier the secret, the classier the blackmailer. Was not Quayle's secret the measure of my worth?

"Your arm still hurts," Joanne said. "Go back to the doctor, any doctor."

"Doesn't," I said.

"You don't go out. You never go out."

"I do so. Just this afternoon I spent two hours in the Morgan Library."

"Work," Joanne said. "I don't mean work. You didn't go out when whoosy-doosy called."

"He's a poet. I told you that."

"You didn't go out when the poet called. Does he scan?"

"Joanne," I said. "Do your homework, listen to music."

She filled the rooms with a partita, the bass not properly adjusted. She was a difficult child.

There I was with time, and I burrowed into my work. I completed my literature search on *Eine Leerstelle*. What a book! Why hadn't I been aware? It had some following, it was read, the object of cultish thoughts.

I might reread it myself. Where was the book? My copy of the book had vanished. It had been on a special shelf between the butterfly book and *A Sharp Left, A Boxer's Night*.

My copy of *Eine Leerstelle* was missing. Where was it? That book was a first edition. My first edition of *Eine Leerstelle* was missing! I searched the shelves, drawers, boxes. It was not there. A slim book with a silver jacket. I had lent it to no one. I did not, as a matter of principle, lend books from my special shelves.

My mother always said, "Stop with the seeking and you shall find."

Still, I was unprepared. The book was not hidden. Like my work, my secret was out in the open, not behind locked drawers, bolted doors.

I had gone into Joanne's room to retrieve my brown sweater, an old moth-eaten affair that I liked to wear around the house when my daughter wasn't sleeping in it. I turned to leave, and there *it* was—on her desk between two elephant bookends. *It* was next to Webster's Collegiate, a supermarket atlas, an almanac from 1958. *Eine Leerstelle* with its paper jacket slightly turned up at the edges.

My special book shelves were not considered as such by my children. To them they were as any other shelves. Had I ever forbidden access? Why would I? Had they ever exhibited an interest?

I opened *Eine Leerstelle*. It had been read. The book had been read. Cautiously, I flipped through the pages. Underlined. Some passages had been underlined. I put the book back between the elephants, thinking maybe Quayle doesn't need hidden microphones when he has in my Joanne a live bug. Was it possible? Was I crazy? Was my Joanne a Quaylite or whatever?

On the third day Quayle began his calls. I knew his voice very well. I analyzed by decibel level, by intonation, by nasal intake of breath. The man was alternately cold, antagonistic, threatening, and clearly narcissistic.

"You will not be able to go through with this," he said. "Do you hear me? My lawyer is at this very moment seeking further counsel."

"Bull," I said, hanging up.

I had been reading that very morning the famous account of Famla's successful career as extortionist. *The threats of the blackmailee are as fog over the Seine*, he wrote.

Famla believed that his success—an income averaging six figures—was due to a careful understanding of the victim. Yes, he called them victims. That had a bad sound to me—a man with a loaf of bread under his arm fleeing. Still, Famla was cool in his advice. Understand the victim, he said, perceive the nature of the secret being hidden. Some secrets are worth only temporary concealment. Might there come a point when the victim says to himself, tell it all—clear the air? This must hinge on the nature of the secret. For instance, the victim reveals the secret—not so bad, everyone says. The blackmailer then becomes victim. So potential blackmailers reflect—by revealing the secret, can the victim gain sympathy? Poor devil, will they say? Imagine carrying that burden. We forgive, they'll say. We forgive you and absolve you of all guilt.

Be realistic, Famla warned.

I was safe. I was realistic. This secret dug deep into

Quayle's being—no peccadillo, no wandering soul, no errant misdeed.

Consider that Quayle only called in the morning, called only to hear my voice. Never when a child might answer the telephone, never to speak to a stranger.

"I can perhaps raise a thousand," Quayle said on the next day.

I could hear traffic noises in the background. "All," I whispered, "all, all, all."

Quayle hung up.

We were engaged in daily warfare. His calls, my replies. "Not now," I often had to say. Sometimes, he cleverly indicated the need to flagellate himself. I was unconvinced. Can a sin travel? It was impossible to know if Quayle had transcended the limits, if indeed he believed himself the author of *Eine Leerstelle*.

He was capable of being supercilious.

"My child," he would begin.

At other times he said, "Woman criminal!"

Once he did not call. The pain was unbearable. I felt paralyzed, unable to leave my rooms. Where was he that he did not call? What was up, an autograph session? Or was he telling someone?

Never, never did I think that Quayle would tell someone. Not even the lady in the yellow hat. He knew that in this he was alone. As was I. So I scrambled some eggs for lunch and took the receiver off the hook.

In the afternoon I went out to engage in the normal activities of a mother of three. I saw first the issue of *Time*. Quayle was on the cover. The sales of the book would swell. It was an idealized Quayle, a noble, pipe-smoking scholar. In the background were swirling mists of seekers. Quayle's Quest, they called it.

Like one practicing acupuncture of the soul, I began a mad search for more evidence. *Newsweek* declared Quayle to be a man for the future, an Einstein, a Kant, a

Hegel. They didn't get his childhood straight, though.

People said, Quayle Qraze Qrows.

The wound on my arm opened and closed. My immune system had become deranged, it seemed.

My newest client, the famous businessman Mr. R., did not invite me to have lunch, although he had scheduled the meeting for one o'clock. Even the room where we met lacked real comfort. It was furnished in grey metal from another period. There was a cup of tea, a brew without character or bite. Nevertheless, we were amiable to each other. I felt that I was suitably, even impressively dressed to meet my client.

"Ah," he said. He had a lisp. "What do you think of my project? Of the way I started. Although I myself have no actual training in the writing arts, I admit to being pleased."

"A fine start," I said. I always practiced diplomacy with clients. "I am glad," I said, "that this is not to be another businessman's biography."

"It isn't?"

"Oh, no. Not good enough for you. A study of inter-relationships. Your family and its influence on business for two hundred years. Encounters with the great."

"Excellent," he said. "We are agreed then."

I nodded.

"The family file room," he said. "Down the hall. My staff will let you in."

We shook hands and parted. I spent three hours in the file room with R.'s relatives, their lives, tax returns, biographies. Big family. Some I had heard about before, through scandal—like that incident with the actress's brother—some through their connections with history. Not a bad bunch really. Generally likable, being optimistic and energetic.

I was given a list of those to be omitted. It had nothing to do with misdeeds or politics. Twenty or so, my client had never liked. Others he would rather forget about.

I was willing to be discriminating, to be selective. A staff member slipped me a piece of paper on which my client had written "Ten Men Who Swayed the World."

"Maybe," I said.

I began that evening with the great Houses of Banking, skated around the scandalous rumors in Hamburg, brought in power and the Crimean War. If I was playing favorites among my client's ancestors, the winner would be C.R. Although not in the direct line of inheritance, C.R. had ambition, he had charm, and perhaps even some intelligence.

He was a man with dark, curly hair and certain unkempt habits. He would have been age fifteen in 1864, the year of the Heleneborg catastrophe. But that was too young, so I made him twenty-five. After the Heleneborg catastrophe, there was still to come the Krümmel factory explosion.

I'm in on the ground floor, C.R. thought.

He offered his assistance to Alfred Nobel. He was heir, the son, to the future that Nobel dreamt about. C.R. was more than ingratiating, he was willing.

"Get me *Kieselguhr*," Nobel ordered.

"Kieselguhr?"

"Yes, yes," Nobel urged.

C.R. nodded. Together they filed patents. The product was named after the Greek *dynamis*.

C.R. was thinking though, C.R. was receiving advice from the uncles. International trusts, they volunteered. That's the way to go.

There was no doubt that Nobel, already a man in his middle years, was a steadying influence upon C.R. "Be skeptical," Nobel advised, "not accepting. Beware of human weakness."

No doubt it was hard on C.R., sitting there while Nobel made a minor adjustment of his pince-nez. Together they checked the locks of the doors at the house on Avenue

86

Malakoff. "Thieves," Nobel said. "Scoundrels everywhere."

"God," C.R. moaned in the evenings, "will I ever be free?"

"What you need," one of the aides advised, "is a touch of the cosmopolitan life. You must find an attractive woman, a bright young woman."

"Yes, yes," said C.R. "A young woman for me."

"No," the aide said, "you've got it in reverse order. Not for you—not yet. For him. For Alf."

It's amazing how when an idea occurred, it seemed to exist independently. There was C.R. hunting for the right young woman, when Alfred Nobel on a week's visit to Baden saw a woman. He was taken with her, with her demeanor, with her affectation of white and black clothing, with her pale skin.

He was not prepared for her, though. "Introduce me," he begged acquaintances.

"Not for you," they insisted.

Alfred Nobel was not to be crossed. He bribed a waiter who arranged the meeting. The woman, Nobel discovered, was the exact opposite of everything that he cherished.

"I don't exactly wish to order you about," he said, "but you are exceedingly difficult."

"Oh, come now, Alfred," Giselle said, casually lifting her skirt above one ankle, "how can I bed down with a man who wants to blow up the world but without annihilating class structure?"

"I want to take care of you," Nobel said.

Giselle shook her head. "Impossible," she said. "Look at you. You do not believe in the masses. You speak out against parliamentarianism. Women's suffrage. You believe in a strong government."

"We could travel," Nobel said. "Germany, Austria, Switzerland, France."

"You want a mistress, a clinger. I dream of peace."

"Life," Nobel said. "A woman should concern herself with day-to-day life."

"A peace congress," Giselle said.

"I dream of a woman to share my life."

"Why not disarmament?"

"You disappoint me," Nobel said. "I can offer you a highly cultivated life, financial freedom."

"The world is dangerous," Giselle said, and embraced him.

C.R. went to Trasker, the managing director of Nobel's plant at Avigliana. "What's up?" C.R. said. "I heard an ugly story."

"So?"

"He was drunk," C.R. said. "Maneuvered this woman, this Giselle, into some corner, flung her skirt over her head, pulled at her clothing, tried to. People watching."

"Tried to?"

"Do it. Had to be pulled off, restrained. People watching."

Trasker shook his head. "I wouldn't think that happened."

"Good," C.R. said, "then I won't."

Nobel returned alone to Vienna. He saw Giselle again a year later. It was in the evening. She was with C.R. Nobel stepped back into the shadow of an equestrian statue of Joan of Arc, and they passed by him without seeing. It was the end of the relationship. "Peace," Nobel wept, and went home to send off a contribution.

Richard stood in the doorway. He didn't mind interrupting, none of the children minded. "Mom," he said, "if you died, what would become of me?"

I was surprised. He was never an inwardly dwelling boy. I did not say I shall not die. "What do you want to become of you?"

"I'd like to stay right here," Richard said. "Joanne can take care of us. She's bossy, but all right."

"I don't think that there's any immediate danger," I said. "But if you couldn't stay here, what then?"

"Maybe at my friend Edward's. The Muchios have a large apartment. Or maybe with Huldie or Rosemary or Grace."

"All right," I said. "I'll bear that in mind."

"I'm going with Joanne," Leon announced. He listened to everything.

"I've reached a decision," Quayle said. I heard a car horn in the distance. "I am going to report you to the authorities. I'm going to do so this morning. Do you hear me, May Alto? You are finished, over, kaput!"

"Sorry," I said, "but there's someone at the door."

"What?"

"The door. Someone at the door." I held the phone away from my ear so that he could hear the buzzer.

"Who is it?" He was whispering.

"I don't know. Goodbye, Quayle."

At least it wouldn't be the man with the coat and the envelope. Could there be more than one? The doorbell buzzed and buzzed, assaulted by jabs.

"Coming, coming," I said.

I opened the door and tried to close it, but the man's foot was too fast for me. He pushed against my weight, and the door opened.

"Hi," Harry said.

"Hell," I said.

"I was in the neighborhood," he said.

"Neighborhood! You're in Colorado, remember? Suburb of Denver, buried in computers."

"Turned out not to be my thing. I called off the trip."

"Called off the trip! Changed the check!"

Harry stared away from me, stared past me. "That's why I'm here," he said. "To explain."

The phone rang. I lifted the receiver on the first bell. "Yes," I said.

"Who?" Quayle said. "Who was it? Who at the door?"

"No telling," I said, and hung up.

"Harry," I said, "go away."

"May," he said, "I want to explain."

"Explain? How can you explain? You can't explain." His suit looked new. His hair was styled.

I, on the other hand, looked terrible—my slacks, my sweater, my fingers pulling at my hair. I looked at Harry. "Please," I said, "please go now."

"Listen," he said, "let me make some fresh coffee. You know I make great coffee. You look all in, old girl. You really look exhausted."

"If I look exhausted, it's because I work, because I am the parent of three children."

"I was being cancelled," Harry said. "May, darling, they were cancelling me all over town. I thought that five would do it. Honestly, I thought that five would. But you know how I was never great with figures. I needed six."

I sat down at the table and put my head in my hands. I could hear the water running, Harry whistling. He was making coffee. He had a secret way, something that he did when his back was to you. His coffee was the best.

The phone rang.

"I'll get it," Harry said.

"In my house I answer the phone." I lifted the receiver. "No," I said, and hung up.

"Who was that?" Harry said.

"My lover."

Harry's cheeks flushed. For some events he displayed an emotion that was involuntary. Or else, I was wrong, and he could blush on cue.

"Can I come to dinner tonight?"

"Only if you want the children to witness your being turned away at the door."

"May, it was circumstances. Circumstances."

Harry poured the coffee into two mugs. He sat down

at the table across from me. We sipped our coffee for a while. We just sat there.

"You're the best woman," Harry said. "You were always the best woman."

We went into the bedroom. The bed had been made that morning and the linen was fresh and cool. Making love with Harry was not a matter of excitement, but there was a certain intensity to it, a continuity. Benjamin had been a wild, unpredictable lover. I had once thought that was a matter of age. We were young and capable of being indifferent to everything but ourselves. I didn't think it was a matter of age anymore. A matter of temperament. Yes, it was just a matter of temperament.

"The kids," Harry said. He reached past me for his watch on the night table. "Late," he said. "I better get up. Shower."

I heard the water running, and I got up and put on a robe. I remade the bed, put on the spread, and smoothed it flat. There was more coffee, and I wanted more coffee.

But first I went into my alcove. There were some lines I had to put down. They would be fitted into the appropriate place later, but I hated to delay such matters.

"Your pale skin," he said.

"I'll admit the attractions of the body," Giselle said, "but you must alter your view of women. Side by side, you said. Together."

"I cannot be radical in my actions," Nobel said.

"An equal," Giselle said, lighting a black cigarette despite his gasp, "is an equal. You have to decide. There isn't a part of an equal. The world is dangerous, Alfred."

Nine

"We'll meet," Quayle said, "at four o'clock on Wednesday afternoon at the long-term parking lot at Kennedy. Are you writing this down? I'm late for a photography session, and I can't repeat. Four at Kennedy. Look for designation one-oh-seven and go directly back to the fence. Wait there. Come in a black car. Have the door unlocked on the passenger side. Do you have this straight?"

"What?" I said. "What?" I could smell the bubbling odors of garlic and leek and carrots and wine. All right, I was cooking that, and the odors were from my kitchen, but they seemed to be exhaled on Quayle's breath.

"Attention!" he said. "Attention! You always struck me as something of a dawdler. I must go now. There are people waiting. Wednesday."

"Wednesday," I repeated.

"Good," he said.

I went into my alcove still carrying my large stirring spoon. I entered everything on my master calendar at once. I wrote, *Q, 4 pm, K long-term, 107.*

Suddenly I could visualize the money. The piles of bills, the bundles of hundreds, all wrapped together like a bale of newspaper. How did you handle that much money? I would have to slip it into many banks, numbered accounts.

I felt like a winner, all right. I felt like the ultimate survivor. What would I do? How would I celebrate? I would make a chocolate torte. My God, what wouldn't I make?

They were coming to dinner. I had invited Grace, Huldie, and Rosemary. In an unofficial way, we took turns. With Grace it was spaghetti and salad. With me, it was unpredictable.

I set the dining-room table with a linen cloth, swept an

overflow of my papers into a cabinet, dusted the chandelier's glass prisms. I used china dinner plates that matched nothing. I had bought them in a thrift shop. They had been a trial run by a manufacturer, an enigmatic pattern that had not been accepted. There were squares, triangles, small v's, and a possible equation.

I felt good, refreshed, stimulated. I would comb my hair, even wear stockings and a dress. Sometimes I trembled with the thought of riches. Just wait until Thursday morning. Thursday morning I would buy something. Never mind what, something heedless and unwholesome.

There were four pots on the stove when the children came home and a dusting of flour on the cabinets. I was wild in my efforts. This was a feast. There would be *two* wines.

"Hamburgers?" Richard asked. "Could we have hamburgers?"

"No," I said.

"You look like a mad chef," Joanne said, leaning against the refrigerator. "Do we have to help?"

"No," I said.

In my mother's house, many women had passed through the kitchen, some to take possession, always five women cooking. Old men sat in the corners sipping tea, making noises, holding a lump of sugar in the teeth. I was open-minded about food. I would try different foods. I had been raised that way. In *A la recherche du temps perdu* Sonya offered the narrator the day's special in the bakery. "The cherry strudel is the best," she suggested. The narrator stamped his foot. "*Madeleines*," he insisted. He was obdurate. Some people will not try anything new.

"I like sauces," Leon said. "You having sauces?"

"Succulent sauces," I said. I leaned over to tickle him, but he dodged away.

"I'm getting out," Joanne said. "Boy, I'm getting out."

"Back for dinner," I said. "Back in time to clean up for dinner."

They were gone again—books abandoned, fleeing the house. It was hard for them. I was always home.

We sat in the living room. The savage interlude of the food over, only the plates and the guttered candles remained. Huldie slipped off her shoes and opened the button on her skirt. "I'm getting fat," she said.

"Yes," Grace said, "you should come to exercise class with me. That'll do it. And cut down on meals like this."

"Now, now," Rosemary said. "You are not fat, Huldie. And the food was superb. Absolutely superb. I should have learned to cook. I should have learned to cook when I was a child."

I had stood at the elbows of many women. I wasn't of their generation, I wasn't to be feared. Like this, they counseled. I learned a lot of secrets. Timing, spice, what was never mentioned in books.

"Too much work," Grace said. "My philosophy is open the can and heat it. Does that hurt? I ask you does that hurt?"

"How long?" Huldie asked me.

"What?"

"The food? How long?"

"I cooked all day."

"I had a dream last week," Rosemary said, "about being in a kitchen."

She had a habit of discussing her dreams. In these dreams she wore thin silk underwear and was always being chased.

"Around the table," Rosemary continued, "he was running around the table. I screamed."

I poured brandy for everyone except Grace. She had another bourbon and soda.

"In winter," Grace said, "my mother wore an old red plaid babushka. I saw a woman with one like that today on the subway. You know the kind with a tablecloth fringe? God, it was ugly.

"When she wasn't watching, I'd unravel a few threads. Afraid to drop them, I'd roll them into a ball and swallow. I wanted that rag to vanish. She had nice dark hair, wavy brown hair. A few threads here, a few threads there, it never seemed to make any difference, the scarf stayed the same size."

Grace stirred her drink with a white plastic swizzle stick that had *The Palmer House* printed in gold letters. She took these sticks from all the places she went, three or four from each place, and she gave them to her friends in little rubberband-tied bunches.

"Well," Huldie said, "I guess I'll drop my bomb. I'm getting married. At least I think I'm getting married. Maybe I'm getting married."

We turned to stare.

"He's a widower," she said. "A friend of the family. Can you imagine, he came with a letter of introduction. He still has an accent. He's from Minneapolis."

I rented a car the next day. A red Ford from Hertz. It was Monday. A few hours, I told the woman in the rental agency. Just for a few hours.

I drove across the Triborough Bridge, minding the lanes of traffic, being very careful. I observed everything I passed. The spread-out countryside of Long Island, the television antennas, each different, on the marching rows of similar roofs. But why were all the windows dark? This was one of those grey afternoons. Where were all the lights? Was there someone in each darkened room staring out and trembling? Or were they sitting there smiling and confident because all was being kept at bay.

I followed the green and white signs correctly. I turned appropriately to the long-term parking lot. What would the attendant think, I wondered, when I returned the ticket? I would be there such a short time.

"Meet all kinds, eh lady," he'd say.

I drove to the sign that said 107. Write your parking area on your ticket, they advised. Back from 107 to the fence I went. The season was between holidays—the lot half-empty. Anyone could have parked reasonably close to the bus stops. Only a handful of cars against the fence.

I saw myself alone there with the passenger door unlocked. I saw possible gullies and ravines.

"Think it through," my mother had said. "Consider motivation."

"You can never be too careful," Aunt Giselle had interrupted.

It was Benjamin whom they were talking about.

"He doesn't even read the newspaper," my mother said.

"No," I said distinctly. "Pay attention to this call—cancel the parking-lot meeting. That meeting is off—not coming."

"No!" Quayle spluttered. "What do you mean not coming?"

"No," I said. "No parking lot, no long-term parking lot, no kind of parking lot anywhere. The city. We will meet in the city."

"I can't be seen with you."

"City," I said. "I have a list of five restaurants—pick one. We'll meet at three-thirty."

"The hell with your list," he said. "Zadkiel's. We will meet there. Table in the center of the window."

Good choice. I admired Quayle's choice. If we must meet in the city, then Quayle understood that it must be publicly. Nothing to hide. Very wise.

"Agreed," I said.

One fact about business—it doesn't stop for personal affairs. This client made an appointment with me one month ago. He came directly from the Secretary. *Take him, sweetheart*, the Secretary wrote. *The military*.

The brigadier-general was wearing his uniform when he sat down across from me at Katz's Delicatessen.

"They think I'm going to a costume party," he said as he looked around.

"Yes," I said.

"What I want," the General said. "Do you know what I want?"

"Yes," I said.

"What?" he said, fingering his insignia.

"The art of creation."

"Exactly. Now I have the material. The story, beginning, middle, end. I want these people to be recognizable but not too much."

"Roman à clef."

"My wife," the General said. "I prepared an outline. Standard outline, indented. My wife and that man."

"Who?"

The General pulled out his notebook and tore off a sheet. He wrote a name. "Here," he said, handing me the paper.

"Him?"

"Yes. One of them. Tell everything, hold nothing back. Afterwards I'll take care of it. I've got connections."

"Roman à clef."

"Yes, I don't see any conflict with form," the General said. "I'll leave first."

I stayed to eat my food, corned beef on rye, celery soda. I read the outline. The General had specified the South. Call the bastard Benjy, the General said. But I had done Benjy already. Detail the assignations, the General wrote. Bodies. Bare. Orgiastic frenzy.

"Make him Greek and fat," the General suggested. "Give them afflictions. Speak of sexual poisons. Tear into them."

"Beginnings?" he wrote. "Are they hard?"

Mother died today.
I couldn't use that again.
Now I was surprised about the lover's identity.
Imagine.
Make him recognizable, but not too much. That was
what the General wanted.
I'd call him C.R.
I wrote on the back of a menu.

Giselle stepped into the cold yellow light of the kitchen.
"There is no doubt that he knows," she said. "No doubt
that the letters have been opened, the calls overheard."
"My God," C.R. said. Was she faithless? This adul-
teress. "There's danger," he said. He saw her dancing—
the gusts of scent, her belly moving, she whirled in the
wind. He wanted her through labyrinths of desire.
"He knows?" C.R. said.
"Yes." Giselle's face was reflected in all the gleaming
surfaces. She echoed back to him.
"You're certain?"
"Yes, he knows."
"Hell," C.R. said. "There is everything that he can do.
He can do everything. He runs it all. I can't even pray. He
knows. The General knows."
"No," Giselle said.
"What?"
"Not him. Nobel."

Ten

"Secrecy must be maintained at all times," Quayle had
warned. "Tell no one."
The question was who was handling whom. Men told
98

women what to do, and women did it. In my appointment book, a large Day-At-A-Glance book, didn't I write *Quayle? Quayle*, I wrote, and a slanted line blocking out the rest of the afternoon. When I vanished, the children would find it.

"Quayle," they'd say.

It was that afternoon, the very one. I could see the restaurant, the appointed table. I was too early. I circled the block like an animal searching for a misplaced cave or a place to put my back against. Coming again each time to the restaurant with its fashionably gold-printed sign, each scrolled letter shadowed with black.

The table in the middle of the window was always empty. The table centered between the white curtains held back by matching ties. Why didn't someone sit at that table specified by Quayle as the table of choice? Was it bugged? Beneath the commercially starched white cloth what? A tiny microphone? Or would he carry it? A voice-activated tape-recorder.

I took up a position at the corner across the street from the restaurant. I pressed my body against a wall. Weren't the police lingering somewhere past that doorway, shivering as I was shivering in a November wind, a wind shaped by curls of debris? Cold enough for you? Isn't that what they would say? Cold enough for you? Getting colder every minute. Why doesn't the broad make the blackmail attempt, and we can all go home? Cold enough for you? In Calgary, they have the chinook. A strange, warm wind that blows clean. We don't have anything like that here.

It was already three-oh-five. No Quayle in sight. If he didn't come by three-fifteen, I would declare it an act of bad faith. But what if he'd been struck down by a gypsy taxi? Nobel Prize winner killed by reckless Spic on eve of great honor.

Yet I lingered there on the periphery of my chosen setting. I was not Quayle's employee. Did I want to scrape and bow? Yes, sir. Yes, sir.

99

"I have raised you," my mother said, "to be a person."

At three-oh-nine, still against my wall, I saw Quayle cross the street. Where had he come from? A limousine stopped across the park? From around the corner? He walked with a measured stride. A man of distinction, a big-time spender. Chesterfield coat with black velvet-edged collar. He was tailored, smooth, neat, warm.

My teeth rattled. I was at the mercy of the cold. Wasn't there a type of woman who always wore a blue sweater under her coat buttoned up against the chill? Beneath my grey reclaimed wool coat could there be a blue one-hundred-percent polyester sweater buttoned up against the winds from the north?

I moved to the left for a better view of Quayle entering the restaurant. He did not hesitate. He sat at the appointed table as if he'd built it with his own hands. Window seat. View of the street. Shrewd bastard. He had a large maroon menu open. I bet the shit didn't even say that he was waiting for someone.

Quayle carried a shopping bag into the restaurant. Not from a store that I recognized. From Quayle's city then. A nice shopping bag. A pure red paper with a galaxy of tiny silver stars. Raised silver stars like bas relief. Of course! In that shopping bag was the tape-recorder and the microphone! What I would say and what he would say damaging forever, the final custody of my children concluded!

Was I actually crossing the street myself? My mouth was a desert, my juices sucked up, distant hammers building a scaffolding, tumbrels rolling.

I opened the thick glass door. The restaurant was small, intimate. The waiter by the door saw me. He wore a black jacket and a bow tie.

"Yes," I said, "there by the window. I am expected."

I removed my black leather gloves, never mind fingerprints. I had been seen, registered. I approached the table.

Quayle looked up. "May," he said.

100

The hesitation, there certainly was a hesitation. He stood up. Reasons were as follows: First, he was a conditioned animal. Second, he did not want to risk offending me. Third, he was putting me in my place. The gentleman rose, the gentleman took the check, the gentleman signified. Crap on the gentleman.

"Hello," I said.

"May," he repeated.

The chair was pulled out and I sat down. The restaurant was empty. The checkroom deserted. Our coats were folded and placed on the empty chair at the table. Even our garments were adversaries, contestants.

"Soup," Quayle said to the waiter.

Never mind that I have just arrived.

"Soup," he said to the waiter. "Mushroom, warm bread. Bring me first a glass of Chablis."

Now I was expected to say the same. To fumble nervously with the clasp of my purse and say the same.

I looked at the waiter and knew, divined, the thoughts in his head. A love affair, the end of a love affair—she's his secretary, there's a wife, another mistress even.

"I'll have a Caesar salad," I said. "Bread, coffee."

The waiter nodded and went away. I called after him. "Yes, and wine. White wine."

"You are looking quite well, May," Quayle said.

Now ours had never been a relationship where my appearance counted. "You look splendid," I said. That was true. I unbuttoned my blue sweater. Beneath there was a black dress.

To be blunt about it, Quayle did not know much about me. Not to imply that such knowledge was necessary—but wasn't curiosity a sign of intelligence?

He nodded, his smile more of a pucker, as if he found the moment a touch sour. Yet no one looking at him would have imagined the truth. He had practiced concealing expression for so long that now he zealously guarded his blankness.

"Good flight?" I said. I thought I was very pleasant.

He made a gesture, a hint of anger, his pride a true companion to his arrogance. "Did you think," he said, "that I came for *this*? I am lecturing tomorrow in the city."

At that moment the waiter approached with two glasses of wine, the food. The wine was not properly chilled. I looked at the waiter. I know my waiters. He was still analyzing the situation. The man's giving her up, he thought. There's definitely someone else already. Probably used to take her to an apartment, a company apartment. Rich men always choose mousey women. No trouble with mousey women. Just peeps from their mousey mouths.

What did he know? Not a bad salad.

I glanced at Quayle. He was staring at his soup.

"Eat," I said. "It'll get cold."

I was in no hurry. Hadn't I blocked out the entire afternoon on my calendar? I would not speed up our meeting.

Let the man eat! Let him leave stinking of food, odor upon odor encircling him.

Quayle was busy assembling the paraphernalia of his thoughts, but his fingers did not drum on the table.

The restaurant, we heard, for it was loudly spoken, closed in less than an hour. Closed until dinner.

Never mind, I smiled at Quayle. I ate my salad, each morsel poised on the tines of my fork. I buttered my hunk of bread—generously, lavishly.

"We will settle our affairs today," Quayle said. He consumed his soup carefully, dipping the spoon away from him. Nothing splattered.

I looked down. Was the salad dressing flying? The coffee dripping down the sides of the cup? Had I spilled my wine?

"I do hope so," I said. "Time is short."

"My time is exceedingly valuable." Quayle looked at his watch.

Not once did I stop eating, not once did I hurry.

"I could have written that book," Quayle said.

"What?"

"I could have written that book," Quayle said. He stared directly at me. For a moment I wondered if I had misjudged the depth of his blue eyes. "Yes," he repeated. "I could have written that book."

I knew what I wanted to say. What I wanted to say to all my clients when bits of raw material like this came up. Why didn't you? Eh, why didn't you? Ran out of ink?

Now all of this came from a woman whose mother never, never held back. "Like it is," she said. "Never spare the sons of bitches."

"Why didn't you?" I said.

"Why didn't I?"

"Write the book. Why didn't you?"

"My life," Quayle said, and now he stared beyond me off into the future and the past, "was full and busy. I was and am involved with the world. I hired you as I would a technician."

"A technician?"

"Yes, my dear," he said. "To put together, to do the mechanics."

I kept up my smile for Quayle.

He smiled back.

"Shit," I said. "A real fair amount of shit. Mechanics? A Tinkertoy operator? Quayle, that book is mine. Never mind whose name is on the cover. You wrote not one line, not one word, not one period, one comma, not even your own name. My book, my words, my ideas."

Through all of this, I kept my voice low. The waiter across the room could certainly tell that a quarrel was in progress, or at the very least one of those discussions between man and woman alone in a restaurant at what was definitely an off hour. Everything was revealed in the way we leaned forward, the firm grips on our beverage containers. Intensity, it said. Intensity and passion. Anger. He was giving me up, breaking away, running back to the wife in the yellow hat. No one for a moment would have assumed that I was the breaker-awayer. Don't tell me that clothes don't matter. The waiter had it all figured. A fling. A momentary weakness in the poor sap's life. Second-rate motel or the company apartment. Was he kinky? Did he dress her up in his wife's nightie?

"Your assumptions, May," Quayle said, "are wild. We spoke together, we discussed."

"I spoke, you jerk! I discussed! You merely nodded your head in knuckle-headed assent."

"*Eine Leerstelle* is my book," Quayle said. "I feel that book, it has entered my system, my soul, my thoughts. Students speak to me about it, it is the subject of many studies, my lectures are filled. My lectures are filled with young men and women who listen to me. I read to them from *Eine Leerstelle*. Would they listen to you? Tell me that? Do you think that they would come in cars, planes, buses, let alone walk, to listen to you? *Eine Leerstelle* by May Alto would be a joke. *Your* book? Never!"

There was fury in his face, real feeling. He had forgotten who he was. His eyes glowed. For a moment, I thought that he really believed it. That he was the rightful author of *Eine Leerstelle*. The rightful author because he looked the part. Now that was right out of the book. That section about facades. Had he read that part?

I swallowed some bread. "Quayle," I said, "back to business. Money."

He put down his spoon, adjusted his jacket, turned his three-quarter profile. "Business? No business, May. I am here out of kindness."

"Up yours," I said.

"Generosity of spirit."

I admired his tone. Quayle hadn't really got this far without some depth to his duplicity.

He lifted the shopping bag, and the paper stars glittered. "You are to take this shopping bag and its contents. This will conclude my kindly gesture on your behalf."

He was pensioning off the old retainer.

I pushed my chair back only slightly. "Dear Quayle," I said, "what is in the shopping bag?"

"A gift," he said, "for past services. Twenty-five thousand. Not strange, properly withdrawn from the bank. I explained it. A good deed, I told them. An act of samaritanism."

I dabbed my lips with the edge of the napkin. "No," I said.

"No?" he said.

"No," I said.

"Take it," he ordered, "or else I'll renounce the prize."

"Renounce it, then."

"You are crazy, May Alto. You are definitely crazy. Twenty-five thousand is more than enough."

"It's peanuts. It's chickenshit. All, Quayle. *All* of it. Half now or cancel your trip to Sweden. The monthly retainer for all eternity."

"I will not meet these demands. Take the shopping bag."

Quayle leaned back and moved his chair away from the table a distance equal to mine. I would have preferred it if he had shown some anger at this point, if he had developed a twitch, spilled his wine, thrown his glass at me. But he leaned back in the classical I-protect-what-is-mine pose.

My mother—found in the room with the pamphlets, the press, the boxes of assorted chemicals—had stared at the arresting officers who wore grey fedoras. "Who?" she had said. "Me?"

"Yes," I said. "You."

"What?" Quayle said.

"I'll go from here to the *Times* or maybe the Washington *Post*," I said.

"Are you so heartless? Would you ruin me? Destroy my life? My children?"

Quayle was doing pretty good. This was no second-rate performance. Had he practiced these words, testing them

105

out, observing his expressions in a mirror? He had everything—the gasp, the slight bubbly break in the voice, the blanched face.

"What were you planning to do for the lecture?" I said.

"What lecture?"

"The Nobel lecture. The one you have to give six months after getting the prize."

Quayle smiled. "I have selected excerpts from the book and two of the essays. They fit beautifully."

"Maybe yes, maybe no," I said.

Quayle moistened his lips. "There's been a dream," he said. "Yes, lately there has been a dream. A dark day in Oslo, midwinter darkness. Suddenly there arises a gold medal. *The* gold medal. It grows bigger and bigger in the sky. It becomes like a sun. I know, even in my dream, that it is my medal. I have but to reach up for it, and there will be immortality."

"Forever," I said.

"Mine," Quayle said.

"Stockholm," I said. "It should be Stockholm."

"In the dream it was distinctly Oslo. The Royal Academy assembled, the Royal Highnesses. A splendid sight."

"Yes," I said. "I can imagine. So get to when they hand you the big bucks."

"I cannot withdraw such a large sum. Even the twenty-five thousand was not easy."

"I have faith in you," I said. "In the meanwhile take your shopping bag with you."

"How am I supposed to continue to withdraw such large sums? Tell me that?"

"Take your banker into your confidence," I said. "There's a woman, tell him. There's a woman with a baby. Guess whose?"

The waiter approached, and we were silent. He cleared the table. He looked at me without pity. She's had it, I could hear him think. The guy has kicked her in the ass. He gave Quayle the check.

106

"Time," Quayle said. "I must have more time."

I reached for my coat. No one offered to help. "One week," I said.

"Two weeks."

"One."

"Agreed."

Eleven

It was logical that Quayle had already ordered the suit. I mean he wasn't going to wear something off the rack. How many chances at the Nobel Prize was he going to get? Good tailoring takes time. Quayle would not be hurried as he examined the coat. "The fit," he would tell the tailor, "must be superb. You must outdo yourself." His wife would be in something crepe. She was a quiet woman.

I had never dreamt about the ceremony, but I could imagine. Our Quayle standing there, humble, wise, accepting. The medal snatched, the feast waiting, the adulation pouring down.

Would Quayle's friends give him a party? Toast him in champagne? Would they wonder, as anybody with any brains would, how such a creep could write a book? *Two* books?

It is my express wish that in awarding the prizes no consideration whatever shall be given to the nationality of the candidates, so that the most worthy shall receive the prize, whether he be a Scandinavian or not.

Was "worthy" like "honest and true"? A light in the darkness, generally notable for its lack of existence?

Could I judge worthy? I considered the list of winners, studied it. All those people since 1901. Some of the names were not familiar. They might never have been remembered had it not been for the prize. The world has fashions in thought. Could *Eine Leerstelle* vanish?

Maybe my mother should have gotten the Nobel Prize. My mother was worthy. There was no time when she put personal self before others. And Aunt Giselle—despite the appetites of the flesh—you couldn't have faulted her causes.

Not me, though. I seldom possessed any worthy thoughts. Not even as a child. I was typical in my expectations. I reflected the human condition. I was, *de facto*, not worthy.

Furthermore, I was sick again. I was sitting on the couch, actually doubled up on the couch, with my knees against my chest. I ached. The pain had started slowly, a mere churning discomfort. Now it thumped away inside me. My forehead was moist, my stomach started to suck violently inward, an implosion of a key organ.

He has poisoned me, I decided. Quayle has poisoned me.

On the eve of my triumph.

Had I looked away? Had I even for a second glanced away from my plate? Had my gloves slipped from my lap? Not necessary. Quayle was in cahoots with the waiter. A potion, Quayle had said. To calm her nerves. Here's fifty dollars. Slip the powder into her beverage. Slip and stir.

I was poisoned. I was sitting there moaning, about to die, cold and clammy. I considered the possibilities. An emetic? The hospital? Was there even time? If only I had made a trip to the safe deposit box. I decided to call someone. I was concentrating on whom to call when the children came home.

I heard the pounding, the noise, the arguments.

"Here!" I called. "Here!"

"Hell," Joanne said. "What's wrong now?"

108

"Ate something," I breathed. "Feel terrible."

"You're white," Joanne said. "You are really white. There's water all over your forehead."

They stood behind her, Richard and Leon staring.

"She's going to die, isn't she?" Richard said. "I know that she is going to die, and we're going to orphanages."

"Different ones?" Leon said.

"Yes," Richard said.

"Shut up," Joanne said. "I'll break your head, Richard, if you say that again."

"I'm not going to die," I said. "I'm just sick."

"You were never sick last year," Leon accused.

"I'll get Grace," Joanne said.

I took a deep breath. "Not necessary," I said. "I'll take a taxi to the hospital, get some medicine, and be back."

"You sure?"

"Yes." I was their sole support.

They moved together like a pack. They got my purse and my coat and led me downstairs. I managed to stand upright and practiced self-hypnotism. I envisioned a distant medal that glowed. I focused on it. Joanne got a taxi for me, and I waved as I left them on the sidewalk, like huddled orphans. The pain in my stomach was now fierce. There was some risk of crying.

Leon was right. Prior to my criminal act, I was essentially a well person. Or was it just chance that my life now seemed fragile? I am alluding to the possibility of psychosomatic disorders, a body filling with guilt. What would follow? A series of unexplained lumps? Thyroid condition? False pregnancy?

The taxi stopped in front of the Emergency entrance. The driver was not interested. I paid him, and he left. I didn't have to pretend any longer that I had come to grips with myself. I permitted myself to walk into the building doubled over, a grotesque twist of a woman.

It was quiet, a quiet time, early evening, middle of the week. Someone led me to a cubicle. Can you undress? I

109

was asked. I thought that someone had asked me that. Yes, yes, I was ambulatory. Did I tell them that?

I put on the gown and climbed up to stretch out on the examining table. All pertinent details had been taken from me. I had a file and a number.

The doctor had my file when he entered the cubicle with the nurse. The file was thick. I had a thick file.

"Ah," said the doctor, "been with us recently, I see."

"Yes," I said. I was a repeater. Three times.

The doctor was examining the file. He was not looking at me. "How's the arm?" he said. I held out the arm. "That wound is not good," he said.

"It opens and closes," I said. "Stigmata."

"What?"

"Nothing," I said. "It's my stomach," I began.

We discussed food ingested.

I was examined.

I knew at once that my body was the recipient of my deceit. Had it not led me down dangerous streets infected with teenagers, mutilated my arm, spurred me on with Harry, torn apart the stomach? My body was paying me back for my failure to be a decent woman.

"Food poisoning," the doctor said.

Ah yes, I thought, right again! But what? The salad? The bread? Unless it was the hot dog purchased earlier from a cart. But no, it must have been that sly bastard, it must have.

I thought that someone might ask why the tears had come, but no one did. The nurse gave me a small box of tissues. "Hurts," she said soothingly. "Hurts."

The doctor patted my shoulder. "We'll fix you up."

They did.

Wait, they said. Sit outside for ten minutes. If you don't keel over, go home. "What you should do," the doctor advised, "is see someone about the arm. That's what I'd do, if I were you."

110

I buttoned up my black coat. I checked my watch. Ten minutes they said, ten minutes it would be. I felt the need to be obedient.

"Yoo hoo!" the old woman called, and beckoned. "Hello."

I knew her. She sat halfway across the room on the bench near the policeman. He didn't look pleased.

"You," I said, and got up cautiously. Slowly, I crossed the room.

"Yes," the old woman said. "It's me. You?"

"Food poisoning," I said.

"Food." The old woman nodded. "Food can be lethal."

"I hardly recognized you," I said. I had recognized the legs.

The old woman raised her one unbandaged arm and pointed to her face, taped into small peaks. The other arm was in a sling, the fingers bound up into a half-fist. "A party," she said. "I went to a party in Short Hills. Good neighborhood. What could happen? Four o'clock in the afternoon, the sky like grey pearls. I took the bus."

"On the bus?" I said.

"The bus going was all right. Bus-to-bus was all right. Coming home at six-oh-five, I said to myself, so far so good, take again a bus. I misread the signals. Without my glasses I took the wrong bus. The driver steered me right. Lady, he says, for NYC you got to go in the other direction. I got off, the sky now black velvet."

"Your friend," I said. "You should have called your friend from Brooklyn."

"Him? Him I don't see anymore."

I looked at the woman, at the white gauze, the puffy, yellow-purple eyes. How had it happened? She was so careful.

"When I reach the Port Authority, it's late. Already trouble. Me, I have on two rings, a fur coat, one watch, my cultured pearls. I'm standing now and waving for a taxi."

I shivered.

"He's got me from behind. He pulls me back to a doorway. My black suede pump twists off. It's a struggle. I'm not resisting, but my weight off-balance is too much for him. Stand up, he says. Meanwhile, pink is in front of my eyes from the blood pressure. In my will everything was left to the daughter in California, and I've changed my mind."

"You're all right," I said. "Anyway, you're all right."

"Took me from chin to ear with the knife," she said. "Stitches. Twenty. They've got him."

"They have him? The man who robbed you?"

The old woman nodded. "In the struggle," she said, "what an uproar, him yelling, me yelling. So meanwhile I pull the old switcheroo. After I jump backwards, I jump forwards, and smack!" She hit her stomach with her good hand. "The knife goes between his ribs." She smoothed down her dress. "Next time," she said, "I wear glasses."

Twelve

Children have to eat. Joanne unbuttoned the first three buttons of her blouse, and I yelled because nothing escaped my notice. Richard and Leon were punished for acts of intolerance. Closets were demolished, raided of dingy garments. Money on the way. "We'll get rid of this, and this," I ordered. I monitored the drawers. There was an avalanche of cleaning. "Filth!" I yelled.

There was a yellowed linen cloth on the table, and it was there that I placed a great feast of hamburgers and French fries accompanied by flows of catsup. For Leon there was a separate dish with pan juices thickened in the style of *nouvelle cuisine* and rich with burgundy, the color like an ancient river's. As they sat and ate, they stared at me, my children. I had overheard their privately expressed doubts. "What's wrong with her?" Richard asked. "Shut up!" Joanne replied.

For days I was testy and querulous. Household objects were things of high hazard. I was a mess. Disequilibrium prevailed.

Was this the criminal mind?

"Can I have a quarter?"

Did I hear that? I yearned to scream absolutely not, get a job, find employment. Yet, trained by habit, my hands searched and found the coin.

And what about the criminal body? My whole carcass began to itch. I decorated my skin with talcum, calamine, cortisone. In the mornings I stood naked in front of the mirror that was nailed to my closet door and looked for rash, welts, signs of insect depredations.

Listen, you can learn to live with anything. So what's a little scratching? I adjusted. Still, suppose the victimizer became the victim. All right, I was a woman with three children, all minors. If it came to that, I would throw myself upon the mercy of the court. The judge perhaps would wear a fedora hat. First offense. Still, a heinous crime—fraud, the public rooked. The judge not inclined to be sympathetic, the judge inclined to be a prick.

So what happened? What happened is that the wound on my arm wept clear serum, and I was overcome with guilt.

Help, I needed help. I tried the encyclopedia, turned to the libraries. I hung around the backs of religious buildings, nodded at women in babushkas, tried to bow, genuflect, and sprinkle with others. Nothing worked.

I thought about the change-of-scene bit. From travel agencies I collected glossy pictures thick with promises. I would take the children away. Switzerland perhaps. There would definitely be enough money.

I called Grace. I didn't use a phone booth, I called right

from home. How often she had bragged about her psychiatrist. "Saved my life," she said. "Marvelous man. Intuitive, not trendy. Do you know what would have happened to me? Do you have any idea? I was nonfunctional. That last divorce just whacked me out, and this wonderful man, a miracle-worker, saved me, snatched me from the wreckage."

My shrink, she always said.

"Grace," I said, "do you still see that psychiatrist?"

"My shrink? My God, yes! I'd sooner give up my soul. What's up? You want to see him?" Grace was not slow.

"Is it bad form," I said, and winced, "to see a friend's—shrink?"

"I'll ask," Grace said. "Was it the poet? I told you he was a jerk."

"Yes," I lied. "I had in mind something fast. A fast treatment."

"Crisis intervention," Grace said. "Good choice. Look, I'll ask him. I'll telephone. How would you say you are—high crisis?"

Oh hell.

"High crisis," I said.

"I'll get back to you," Grace said. "Stay home, drink tea, no booze."

"No booze," I agreed.

Did I curl up in bed? No. I went back to work. I took a bus to the New York *Times* to collect some clippings. The man sitting across from me wore a white shirt under a thick sweater, his beige trousers creased, only slightly soiled, his hair combed, the face old and badly shaven. Brown socks and no shoes, a small hole in the right sock. No shoes! Over his brown socks, he had no shoes! I mean, this is the kind of world I travelled in.

I looked at the other passengers. Did they not notice? Were they just pretending not to stare, afraid of what it might bring? The grey-haired woman seated next to me,

114

so compact and neat, was eating her crumpled tissue. She stood up and crossed the aisle, to reseat herself next to the man with no shoes.

At the next stop a woman and a child got on. The child pulled at the woman's arm. The woman smiled. "Yes, darling?" she said.

"I want to read to you," the child said. "We got a new reader."

"Yes, darling," the woman said.

The child opened a book.

"*See,*" the child read. "*See Giselle. See Giselle run. Throw the ball, Giselle. Throw the ball. Catch the ball, Sonya. Come, Trasker. Come.*"

I got up and rang for my stop.

The clippings were about extradition both to New York State and to the United States. The children would be taken care of, thank God for friends. Now I had to save myself. Was any place safe? I picked up an atlas on the way home.

Grace called within the hour. Some people would do anything to avoid Grace on the trail, Grace on the sniff.

"Bingo!" she said, her voice high with elation. "He'll see you. You are very lucky, May. You don't know it yet, but you are very lucky. No more long-term cases, he said. But he was willing to do a favor for me. It's crisis, I said."

"How crisis did you tell him, Grace?"

"Brink," she said. "I wasn't sure how booked up he was. On the brink, I said. Mother of three, I said."

"When?"

"This afternoon at four. He's in the building directly across from my Cousin Ida. You know?"

"Yes," I said.

On the brink. I better leave off the makeup, go in black, mess up the hair. I didn't have the nerve to cancel the appointment. But already I hated the idea.

Better to have taken the money.

"Don't hold back," Grace advised. "Open your heart to the man."

It was a comforting thought—dump the cargo, lighten the load. But the act itself, actually going to a psychiatrist, would empty me of every impulse of confession. Not unless I could go hooded.

I had thought of confession as a pillow, a quilt you sank back on, the comforting face, a Yahweh of the mind. My earliest nastiness, I'd begin. He'd absolve, I'd tell more. Backs of cars, Indian villages, dank cellars. Only the good stuff.

My desire to tell all just went. A passing inclination towards penitence. I wasn't going for absolution.

That's the criminal mind at work. I didn't want to tell anyone after all. I didn't want liberation. I preferred guilt. Maybe I would become a student of hatha yoga. How the hell had I expected to confess to Grace's shrink? In the place where once a week Grace sat and said, "My mother."

At three I dressed for the session. Black slacks, black sweater. Face scrubbed raw into a healthy pink. I took one glass of wine to deepen the shade to a natural, pale crimson. The scent on the breath had a nice brink-quality. Then it was go, pop along. Grace after me.

I rode the subway to find Dr. Morganstern. I sat next to a man in a raincoat who mumbled. I didn't know his motives. He mumbled, "Don't care. Let them."

Take my appointment, I would have offered. Go. Let them bill me.

But the man got off too soon, leaped from his seat, raced to the door. At once he appeared rational, hurried, important. I too left the subway at the right stop.

This was a better neighborhood than mine. Look at Morganstern's building. Sleek. Probably not filled with petition-signing rent-controllers. Ground-floor apartment, Grace had once said. Office and apartment. There was a separate street entrance with a small brass plate properly oxidized to green. Discreet. I regretted not having brought a yellow pad and some pencils. I might have wanted to take notes.

I didn't want to go in. My breath came in chilly gasps. He was Grace's doctor. That link with Grace was what propelled me forward. In my mind I was pulling a U-turn, no traffic cop in sight. I would have gone to a telephone, coughed repeatedly as I spoke, and claimed a rare disease that made the appointment, all appointments, impossible. I knew many diseases. But there was Grace, more fearsome than the unknown doctor.

I touched the buzzer. Someone inside replied in kind. I opened the door and entered the waiting room. I was alone. In this one-to-one field of work, you don't have to worry about a collection of people staring up at you. I looked around. It wasn't bad. The room had character. When the premises were promising, my mood improved. I admired the vinyl-covered chairs—all green. The nice old rug, grey and dirty. The plant in the corner, bound in darkness, never needing water. Even the magazines were mysterious in origin—offering tips on child care, views of the South Seas, recipes. The two narrow octagonal windows were rain-splattered and dried with streaks of street dirt. I sat right down and read about gourmet feasts, three wines, a table setting with four forks.

A chime sounded, soft, good tone. Was it a warning that my time had come? Time to stop all activities and rise up before the entrance of the Good Shrink Morganstern. "Move swiftly," my mother said, "act innocent, and always let them speak first."

The inner door opened, a solid door, no apartment hollow-core. You couldn't hear confessions through that door. "May Alto," Dr. Morganstern said, and indicated that I was to enter the other room.

He was better than I could have imagined. Where had Grace found him? He had short brown hair, wore a

117

Harris tweed jacket, a wool-knit tie. And glasses, he had brown-rimmed glasses.

In the inner room was a genuine mahogany desk, another plain rug made grey, a lamp on the desk with a green glass shade. It was very real.

Dr. Morganstern held out his hand. "May," he said, "call me Morganstern."

Nobody's perfect, I thought.

He motioned, and I sat down. I was braced for what would come. I hated filling out forms—when did I have mumps?

"Crisis," he said. "I understand you have a crisis."

I liked him again.

"Yes," I said. I leaned back. The chair wasn't too comfortable, and the middle spring hurt the neural arch of one vertebra. "I am planning to commit a crime," I said. Never mind the poet.

"Planning?" he said. "Haven't done so yet?"

"I'm in the middle of it," I said. "Non-violent."

"What is the exact nature of the crime?"

"Blackmail," I said. "No money has changed hands yet."

"And you attribute your crisis to a buildup of stress—incurred during the act of planning?"

The planning wasn't too bad, actually.

"No," I said, "I don't think so."

"There were pangs, then—the crisis is that you don't want to go through with this crime. You want to stop."

I shook my head. "Definitely intend to go through with it. Beginning to end. It never occurred to me to do otherwise. The crisis is that I feel bad about doing it."

Morganstern listened. "I hear," he said, "more than you are saying. I hear that you do not wish to commit this crime. I hear that you want to stop now before it becomes too late."

Quayle, I heard, *I'm going to get you.*

"How much," Morganstern said, "do you want to tell me about this?"

118

Not the name, I decided.

"I could give you the gist of the problem. Yes, I could do that," I said. We could skirt the edges without the core. "Tell me," I said, "do you record?"

"Tape record?"

"The sessions."

"No."

"Any breaches of confidentiality?"

"No."

"I write for people," I said.

"Ghost?"

"Sort of."

Morganstern nodded. "And now," he said, "you are blackmailing one of these people."

"My client," I said. "But I want you to know that I have never done this before. Have never even been tempted. I accept my fee, and that is all, no matter what happens to the material, no matter how popular it becomes."

"You are struggling with your psyche, attempting to cover up your discontent."

"Whitewashing?"

"Yes," Morganstern said. "You are trying to see yourself as pure, your motives as the best."

"Maybe," I said. "But I never did this before. It's just this one instance. This one time when it got to be too much. I just couldn't bear this one."

That didn't bother Morganstern.

"You like your work?" he said.

"Definitely. It's a great pleasure."

"Do you think we should consider the possibility that this blackmail attempt is the outward manifestation of new feelings about your work? Negative feelings? Or old feelings, previously suppressed, that are now escaping?"

Did I consider that? No, I would not blackmail anyone else. I knew that. Just this once. Just for the fucking *Nobel Prize*!

"Wrong track," I said. "I mean I really do like my

work. Tremendous satisfaction. I would never, never go back to anyone for more money."

"This particular client," Morganstern said. "You hate this client?"

Hate Quayle?

"Probably not," I said. "I mean, hate is strong. Probably dislike, or a trifle despise."

"Let's see," Morganstern said, and began to count down on his fingers. "Possibility number one, you are threatening to reveal more information about the subject. Possibility number two, you will expose your role as co-author. Possibility number three, you possess knowledge of a sexual nature."

Three strikes.

You're out.

"Wrong," I said.

He was not pleased.

"In your work," Morganstern said, "you meet with people, obtain their material, and write it up—correct?"

"Occasionally," I said. "But most often they don't give me any material. In fact, that is my specialty. My clients come to me for my creativity, my ability to make something out of nothing."

"Many clients?"

"Many."

"Let's go to a neutral client—one not being black-mailed. Can we discuss a neutral client?"

I stared past Morganstern's head. He had the wall of book shelves. They all had that. As I expected, I saw some of my books there. I took a deep breath. "Confidentiality?"

"Yes," he said. "And I want you to know that I am very interested in books, collecting, reading. My mother belonged to the Book-of-the-Month Club. That is one of my earliest memories. Later, there was the library, a red-haired librarian."

"For instance," I said, "behind you."

Morganstern swiveled. "Which one?"

"The blue and yellow cover. *The Terrors of an American Beauty*."

"Yours? How much yours?"

I crossed my black legs. I perceived a temporary disturbance in Morganstern, but I had committed myself. This I could confess.

"It was an assignment," I said. "My bread and butter, you see. Not an unusual assignment. I wouldn't want you to think it was an unusual assignment. After the telephone call from her husband, I met the two of them in their lawyer's office. Her husband was clever, her manager. We said hello, we shook hands. The husband spoke. He was the one who suspected the truth, that her beauty would fade away. Already there were the lines. He wanted me to give her depth. To open the way for character parts. Write up her life, he said. Make it interesting."

"Interesting?" Morganstern said. "Interesting?"

"Did you think it was? Sure, I said to the husband. She didn't seem terribly concerned, kept wandering around the room. Perhaps her troubles had already begun, the way she plucked at the drapes."

"She was magnificent," Morganstern said.

"Well, that's it," I said.

"That's it? What do you mean that's it? You spoke to *her*, didn't you? Asked her questions about her life?"

"Not really," I said. "Actually, we met that afternoon for about a half-hour—there was the money to discuss, the lawyer. They gave me some photographs, the fact sheet from the studio. I never saw her again."

"Just a moment," Morganstern said. "What do you mean you never saw her again?"

"I never saw her again."

"Then how did you find out about the schools? The father and the soothsayer? That dance in Liège?"

"Schools," I said. "Schools are schools. I mean, we were all young once. It was a matter of selection—the math teacher, the cheerleaders. That unpleasant dance. Who doesn't remember the unpleasant dance? Someday I'll tell you about mine."

I thought that Morganstern may have moaned.

"God," he said. "That's been much discussed, that book. Discussed, analyzed. Her conclusions—those conclusions about the place of beauty in American society. I've used them."

I was definitely interested and leaned forward. "Were they useful? The conclusions, could you apply them?"

"My patients," Morganstern whispered. "I have some very beautiful patients."

Wisely, I said nothing

"Tell me more," he insisted. "Go on."

The man was a pain-collector. "More?" I said. "About her? After all, I only saw her that one time. On the fact sheet, there wasn't much worth using. They tend to exaggerate. But listen, she was very beautiful, even in person. Not articulate, non-vocal, in fact—but beautiful. Her husband answered for her. I was on my own in this. Do it, the husband said. Not *as told to*—no, he said, my wife will be the sole author. Spill her guts, he said. So I began. I switched the birth from Kansas to Ohio."

"Never," Morganstern said, "can I quote from this book again."

"But the conclusions," I said, "can't you apply them?"

"What? Yes, *No*! You never saw her again? Are you certain? She read the manuscript?"

"He did, the husband. All right, he said. They mailed the check. The check was big, it was huge—money. I never blackmailed them. I never thought to, not even with the book club, the movie. Did I ever think of getting more? I did not."

Morganstern tapped lightly on the desk with his ballpoint pen. "Then it's not about her—how could it be? It's written by you. It is basically not about her."

"Oh, no," I said. "Of course it is about her."

122

"How can it be about her if it is not about her?"

I pulled at my hair, I pushed at my hair. "It's as much about her as anything could be. If she later paid enough attention, if she absorbed the material, then it's about her."

Morganstern leaped from his chair. He was an agile man. He jerked the book from the shelf. Bits of paper fell from the pages like crumbs on a forest path. The book had the loose, easy look of a volume well read.

"For instance," he said. "The Berlin pages. That time when she was in Berlin when she finds that her image in mirrors has begun to fade."

"Yes," I said.

Is that me in the mirror?" Morganstern read. "*The quicksilver glass? I think that it is me, but how indistinct grows the image. The face vanishes into the future. Sonya is the only one who does not doubt the truth of what I say. Oh Sonya, yes, let me speak to you about Sonya. That woman whom I met on the street outside the Auerhof Hall, her dress and shoes muddied. She was handing out pamphlets, hawking them, though they were free. Did she see me? As I am? 'Come,' she said to me, 'your image disappears because it grows into itself. Be outward-thrusting. Think of the world. Yes, girl, think of the world.' I wanted to please her, so I bound my hair, removed all makeup, and next day joined her in the street. She was not pleased. 'Be as you are,' Sonya said. 'Who do you think you are kidding?'*

"'You're a distraction,' Sonya said one day. 'You mean well, the heart is properly positioned, but you are a distraction.' Giselle, another member of the group, took me aside. 'You are what you see,' she said not unkindly. She took me that night to a restaurant called the Fond du lac. There was a jolly group at the table where we sat, and Giselle introduced me that night to Herr M. I left the cause forever."

"Those people," Morganstern said. "She knew those people."

I stretched forward. "Who can tell?"

Morganstern stared at me. "This woman—this Sonya—how did you find out about Sonya? Tell me that? Sonya is the classical example of the mentor."

"My mother."

"Who?"

"Sonya is my mother."

Morganstern checked the book. "It says," he read, "*Sonya was twenty-nine*. If Sonya was twenty-nine—and we're talking twelve years ago—how could she be your mother? And Giselle, Sonya's friend Giselle—your mother too?"

"My aunt."

Morganstern was trembling. I saw the arms move in a staccato beat beneath the tweed. He put the book back on the shelf upside down.

"You never contacted these people—the actress or her husband—again?" he said.

"Never," I said.

Morganstern walked back to his desk. He sat down. We waited. Composure took time. I thought he murmured, "Her breasts, her legs, her thighs."

"We won't discuss this client again," Morganstern said. "The neutral one. The other one, the one you're blackmailing, has a similar situation, I presume. Although special, more rewards."

"He wasn't like *her*. Imagine thinking that. Biographies are one thing, like adventures, but this was different. It wasn't his life, after all."

"This person," Morganstern said, "the one you want to blackmail—how different from the others? Did he attack you, treat you in a gross manner, refuse to pay you?"

Quayle had a fine tweed jacket woven in an ancient Druid pattern. "I'll say goodbye to you, then," he said.

I must have worn my raincoat.

124

"Yes," I said. "Goodbye."
I folded the check.

"Slime-mold," I said. "Quagmire."

Morganstern didn't respond. Perhaps I didn't say it. I thought about Freud and his lover. Freud and Giselle in Charcot's house when he did her analysis.

"This person behaved all right," I said. "No, I cannot say that the work relationship was difficult."

"And yet," Morganstern said, "you want to blackmail this person. How long have you considered doing this? Years?"

"Weeks," I said. "Two and a half."

Morganstern nodded. He was solemn. Forgotten was his previous outburst. "The glass-of-water theory," he said.

"What?"

"The glass-of-water theory. You can pour water into a glass, more and more, but the amount that can be safely poured into the glass is finite. Suddenly you add one more drop, and all the water overflows."

"Yes," I said.

"You are angry," Morganstern said. "Not good-natured, not adaptable—angry."

"Yes," I said.

"The person you are blackmailing."

"The blackmailee."

"The blackmailee—how does this person react to the attempt?"

"Fury," I said, "despair, arrogance."

"Accedes to your demands?"

"Will," I said. "The person will accede, because the person faces ruin."

Morganstern did not visibly react. "But you do not want to cause the destruction of a fellow human being, do you?"

"Never did it before. Not even to my husbands. A big

125

responsibility. I feel as if I'm spoiling a perfect attendance record."

"You mean," he said, "that you are your image."

"What?"

"You are obsessed with this crime you are planning—you are choking on it, unable to do anything else."

I was one hundred pages into the General's very own story, already up to the place where the wife goes to the astrologer, and two hundred and ten pages into C.R.'s pursuit of G. in California. Never mind the other works in progress.

"Actually," I said, "I am still productive. Crime or no crime, my family has to eat. There are responsibilities. Like Goethe said, I don't watch my own thinking."

Morganstern shifted his weight. "You feel this person deserves it?"

I envisioned a vicious uppercut to Quayle's groin. "Wham!" I said, gesturing with my good arm.

"May," Morganstern said. "I want you to meditate until we meet again. I'll want to see you in three days, because the crisis level is so high. I want you to meditate about what this course of action means to you, to your family. Is it worth it? I want you to think about breaking away from the behavior that has led to your anger."

The pile of money, I decided, would be enormous. A bale of it. Enough to fill a bathtub. Here, Quayle would say. Here, female!

At this point, I was watching my own thinking.

"Listen," I said, "I have to tell you. I will go through with it."

"Along with meditation," Morganstern said, "I advise a less strictured view of the world. Go out, be with others, help others. What you need is *Gemeinschaftsgefühl*."

"*Gemeinschaftsgefühl?*"

"Thoughts of society."

"Says who?"

"We'll see," Morganstern said. "Go home. Meditate."

126

I put on my coat. Morganstern helped.

"Goodbye," I said. "Tuesday."

Morganstern pushed at his hair. "Are there," he said, and coughed, "are there other books here that you've done? I mean, do you happen to see any?"

I looked at the shelves. From across the room you couldn't see everything. "The green cover," I said. "There, third shelf from the bottom, five or six books to the left. That's one. *Ethos, Pathos, and the Portuguese Woman*."

"What?" he said. He danced on tiptoe.

"Such a decent man that one. Mr. B. came to me for a book about his wife, his mother, and his sister. He'd give it to them for a present. His mother sent me a sweet note afterwards. What a surprise, she said. My son's a darling, she said. I never met the wife or sister."

"God!" Morganstern said. "Ethnic grouping in mainstream culture."

"Family spirit," I said. "The peaks and valleys of life."

"Those women," Morganstern said. "The family feasts, the Easter egg hunt, the long conversations. The strange clashing machinery that no one could locate. The mother's lover—the time he hid in her cellar. That time with Trasker during Lent. The woman Giselle, who arrived late one night. What about the girls? That child Grace?"

I nodded. "I was particularly moved when the police came for the mother," I said. "No one knowing how it could be."

"Wait a minute," Morganstern said. "Hey, wait a minute! This Giselle—what Giselle is this?"

"A Circe," I said, "in the Judaeo-Christian tradition."

"Who is Trasker?"

"A sort of uncle."

"God," Morganstern said. "May, go."

The street lights weren't on when I left the office. A malfunction perhaps. The early northern evening was as grey as the week-old slush that slowed the feet. There were few people walking about. A man was chasing a boy about twenty. The boy shouldn't be running around without a coat, with only a grey scarf about his neck. The man had a two-by-four in his hand. "Wait till I get you!" he yelled.

A girl in a yellow coat shook her head as she walked down the street. "Shit," she said and kicked at the snow. "Oh, shit," she said.

I checked in all directions before starting out. It looked like a good street for a mugging.

Thirteen

I had always considered my home a haven, a place where you could seek refuge. So I did not consider it impossible to meditate there. I tried, sitting very straight in a hard wooden chair, listening to the cries of my children as they stormed towards me. I heard Richard screaming something about Burger King. Leon yelling "McCheese," and Joanne telling them both to shut up. You think it's easy to meditate?

But that was not all. In came Grace, the bloodhound. She'd sniffed me out again. "I am aware," she said, "that it is not good form to ask someone how their session with their shrink went, so I will not ask that question. I just want to know what you think of Morganstern."

"He's acceptable," I said.

"Acceptable! Morganstern is perfect! He has a grasp of theory that cannot be matched. He is without baloney, May. Totally without baloney. He does not go in for any of that spiritual tradition stuff, no great theories of the past. The man is usable."

"I like him," I said.

"And he'll help you," Grace said. "Stick with it, and you'll be all right. Later, we'll introduce you to someone. What are friends for?"

Trouble came immediately to mind.

The phone rang. Joanne answered it. "For you," she called. "It's the poet."

"Hang up!" Grace shouted.

"Christ, Grace," I said, and went to the phone.

The poet's name was Peter. "Hi, May," Peter said.

"Hi," I said.

"I have given your question some thought," Peter said. "You should begin meditation without tools. Without outside supports. Seek a harmonious place for yourself."

"What question?" I said. "All you did was call this morning, and I said that I couldn't talk because I was meditating. Not a question."

"It's a matter of intuition," Peter said. "Is it possible to have me as a guest for dinner?"

"Grace," I said, "would eat you alive."

"I'll chance it," he said.

"No," I said.

I found myself loitering outside Grand Central Station. Not unusual under normal circumstances, except this was the fourth time in one week. What for? Let's face it, I probably wanted to run away. Maybe a journey. But mothers did not idly start journeys. Journeys had to be planned, schools consulted, holidays, three sets of individual schedules. No, I could not begin a journey. There were only a few days left to wait, one more trip to Morganstern, one trip to Quayle. Thus, we divide our weeks, we women, divide them by the men.

Then came the shock! Quayle, who was not to be heard from for three more days, sent me a letter. Imagine, a letter from Quayle! Quayle had written something on paper. I saw it as an omen, some word from the fringe of darkness.

The visions and colors of my period of hallucinatory pain staged a recurrence. What I had here was a drugstore-style number-ten envelope—crisp, not expensive. I opened it, slitting the end neatly with my fingernail.

Quayle was starting something, Quayle was launching a plot. I thought of the letter as a link between cause and effect. What the hell was he up to?

Dear May,
    First of all, I cannot be reached. Incommunicado. Lectures are taking me here and there, the itinerary complex. Nevertheless, we must meet. Let our meeting take place on Monday at the address below. Come at three in the afternoon.
                                                                    Q

Blue ballpoint, the dot over the *i*'s a half-circle, Quayle had written a letter. Quayle in the act of letter-writing.

The address was an apartment building, the East Side. The apartment number was 15B.

Should I go armed?

The meeting date, if I kept it, was for the next day. It drove all other thoughts from my mind—Morganstern, meditation, and so forth. How would I carry the money back—in a wheelbarrow? A suitcase?

I made a quick trip to the bank. In the safe deposit box that I had rented but which was empty, I put the letter about Quayle, the Q letter, and my holographic will.

That evening I kissed each child in turn and never spoke while they watched television.

"I told you," Richard said to his sister when they met in the hall opposite my bedroom door. "I told you that she is going to die."

"Die nothing," his sister said. "Worse, much worse— marry Peter Cottontail."

"Who?"

"Shut up."

I worked that entire evening. Worked for the General, who was no absentee client. Some of them never leave you alone. He had sent me a list of suggestions. Set a trap, he said. That G. is terrific as my wife. So I wrote a trap.

The room wasn't dark. Rather, it was well lit. In the corner was the curtained booth. Giselle didn't hesitate, although she suspected the degree to which this was a set-up. Trust the General to do it up right. But then he had enough money. What couldn't you do right with enough money? You'll feel better, he'd said. A private sanctum, he'd said. Confess!

Giselle went behind the curtain and sat.

"How long has it been since you last confessed?" the man asked.

"Five, maybe six years," Giselle said.

"Have you any sins to confess?"

"I don't trust my husband. I believe that the General is spying on me."

"Hush."

"What?"

"Are you performing the conjugal act?"

"I do it fairly often. He has genital organs, I have genital organs."

"Be more explicit."

"I know what you want," she said. "You want the description of a feast. Decadent food, odors, perhaps a rotting peach forgotten. You want a dark room, a Tekke rug on the floor like a lake, the color of the deepest blood-red flooded with cartouches and scrolls of gold and green and black, the fringe extra long. You want flesh like flames. Languor, fainting, desire spreading like fog. You want entangled legs, hands on asses, more than bodies, an endless spending of lascivious energy. You want that?"

"Yes," the voice said.

"His hands foraged through my body. A wilderness, he said. He approached the frontiers of my body like an N. Bumppo in heat."

"The General did that?"

"Where did you get that idea? Never with the General. It was not with him. But I assure you that the family was opposed."

"More details."

"Listen, I'm not getting into pornography. You don't have a back door, do you? Some place where I could hide—downstairs, maybe?"

The next morning I washed my hair. I sprayed with perfume. The way I dressed for this—the final, the ultimate meeting with Quayle—was the way I had dressed for my first meeting with R. I tried a silk scarf around my arm. I thought it looked debonair, sexy. What else could I do, anyway?

How great were the dangers? Who could tell? It all depended upon the size of the East Side apartment, the number of exits, who controlled the situation.

Did I not control the situation?

"Don't let them get behind you," my mother would have advised.

I planned to arrive on time, never mind the advantages of arriving late. My heart—my entire body—throbbed with dangerous rushes of blood. I stepped into a taxi and headed towards *My Prize*.

The apartment lobby was marble and chrome. There was a doorman, an intercom. I was announced. "One minute," the doorman said. "Your name?" I gave my name and was led to the elevator.

There were muted roses on the carpet that lined the corridor of the fifteenth floor. Huge, fat roses in the style of French water-colorists. Vague fluffs of white clouds on the wallpaper.

The door to 15B was a trifle ajar. I could see that Quayle was standing behind it ready to close the door at the first sign of hooliganism.

"May," he said and opened the door to its widest. "Come in."

"You've beaten the deadline," I said. There are scents that you know, feel. The animals were right. The olfactory sense aroused was not to be dismissed. This wasn't simple sweat glands pumping, forehead dripping. This was a complex mixture of pituitary and adrenal. Quayle smelled of layers of deception. My guard was so strong that I almost entered the apartment on tiptoe. Was this what the waiter was expecting? The company apartment. Where did Quayle get this apartment?

The furniture was sleekly made. French reproductions, an expensive suite. Hall, living room, couldn't see beyond.

"I haven't," Quayle said. "The deadline." He was in blue blazer, gold buttons, maybe real gold buttons, grey slacks, blue shirt. "I thought that we should talk again."

I looked around for a bottle of wine in a silver-plated cooler. There wasn't one. At least not in any of the rooms that I could see. Quayle was already slipping the coat from my shoulders.

"I don't understand," I said. The things people say. I understood all too well.

"May," Quayle said. "This is for both of us an unfortunate situation."

Manipulative therapy, I suspected. The situation as described by Trasker *et al*. at the American Psychoanalytical Meeting in 1936.

"I am certain," he continued, his voice pitched extremely low, "that we never intended such circumstances to alter our lives. You risk, you must realize, difficult proceedings, terrible consequences for attempting to obtain funds in such a manner. I, I admit, suffer the embarrassments of public exploitation."

This is what happens when you're around certain people. Never would such emotions have been expressed in *Eine Leerstelle*. Why didn't the man read the entire book?

"Nuts," I said. "It's pay up or face the headlines."

There was suddenly a hopeful sign, an involuntary

upward motion of the left side of the mouth towards the cheek. The zygomaticus muscle was alive. But the movement was transitory. It never developed into a full-fledged tic.

Awareness came to him, nothing passed to his face. I had to give him credit. His climb to the top wasn't entirely luck. He had the street-smarts. Could he even be intelligent?

"Sit down, May," he said. He indicated the couch.

The down cushions sank low, encapsulating me. Quayle at once bounded over and sat down one cushion-length away. We sat in silence. I did not meditate. Instead, I viewed his profile again. He had a good Roman-coin profile. Most people would immediately assume that a blackmail attempt involving this man had to be sexual. He was handsome, wise-looking. There were certainly some *Eine Leerstelle* followers capitulating somewhere, brain groupies.

"May," Quayle said, turning to give me the three-quarter view, "these are difficult times for a woman. We all know that too well. The world moving down new paths. Are you still divorced?"

Scumbag.

"Yes," I said, "I'm still unmarried."

"And the children? You have three children?"

"You want to hear my social security number?"

"Difficult." Quayle shook his head. "Alone. The days. The nights."

"I can't stand company," I said.

"We grew up in the same time period," Quayle said. "We lived through the same world traumas."

If he had written *Eine Leerstelle*, we wouldn't have been here.

"May," he said, "life has a future for both of us. I can be in a position to help you. I have often thought of you. You and your children can leave New York at last. The crime, the dirt, the ugliness. I can even find employment for you on my staff. We needn't be adversaries. I need an assistant."

134

He was looking at me now. The blue eyes darkening. He moved his arm. It slithered across my lap. He had a long reach. His hand clasped mine and pulled it towards the neutral central cushion.

"Would you like a glass of wine?" he asked as his fingers tightened over mine.

So I wasn't to be disappointed, after all.

"Sure," I said.

Quayle let go of my hand after a small but definite squeeze. He vanished into the room beyond.

Did I run away? Are you kidding! I sat there waiting. When he returned, it was with a chilled bottle of Riesling wrapped in a small towel. In his other hand he carried two glasses.

"My dear," he said, and poured some wine for me. He poured some for himself. "Let us toast," he said.

I took one glass. "To big bucks," I said.

"Let us drink," he said, "to our new relationship."

"Relationship," I repeated. The glasses touched.

The meeting had begun at three. There were no lamps lit in the room. None needed. Bright light everywhere. I estimated that by four we'd be in shadows.

"May," Quayle said. "I am direct in my manner. I want to go to bed with you."

Did I want to go to bed with a Nobel Prize winner?

Hell, did he?

The squares and circles of his thoughts settled into their accustomed slots. His fingers edged up my arm, a soothing, light pattern, a quick brush across the breasts.

'I'll just call my answering service,' he said. "One second."

I sat there and thought of girls in plaid skirts, girls in jeans, girls in grey business suits. I mean this was a real famous man. He showed them exactly what they were, not hot items, merely potential puddles of lust. Dipsomania, paranoia, nymphomania.

"My messages?" he said.

What did the voice reply?

"Yes," Quayle said.

"Yes," Quayle said.

"Repeat," Quayle said.

"May," Quayle said after completing his call. "Let us go."

I nodded. I expected that this would be rather different from that long night when Bloom went to bed with Giselle in *Ulysses*. No sounds of Dublin here, no parallels to Homer. As it was written, I believe, Bloom said, "I can compare you with no one." "Be a luv," Giselle said, "and do keep quiet."

Quayle came back to the couch, took my hands, and pulled me up. He kissed me lightly on the forehead and walked me into the room that I had not been able to see before.

There was a small bookcase next to the bed. I examined the books. There was a butterfly book, *An American Tragedy,* a book on common ailments, a book on pain, two novels from previous years. "There's no copy of *Eine Leerstelle?*" I said.

"What?" Quayle was annoyed.

"No copy."

"Let us not talk of such matters," he said. "May, we have the afternoon before us. And later, more."

"Whose apartment is it?"

"A friend's," Quayle said. "An important person."

"Who?"

Quayle reached for the top button of my blouse. "Names are not important. A friend—a man—called him R."

That accounted for it. That there was no copy of *Eine Leerstelle.*

Quayle was turning back the spread. Then he duplicated the fold with the sheet and the blanket. He took the time to be careful. Did the bed have to be remade?

"You're very attractive, May," Quayle said. "A woman of qualities."

"Thank you," I said.

We removed our clothes. I placed mine on a Louis Quatorzième chair in the corner. Quayle hung his on wooden hangers in the empty closet. Naked, I arranged myself on the white sheet.

In truth, he was more skillful than I would have guessed, more imaginative. He had picked up a lot from today's youth. Still, we weren't children on that bed. Were pine needles clinging to my back?

"Ah, May, May," he whispered.

"Well, old girl," he said as he rolled off. A nice bit of camaraderie. "More wine?"

Without waiting for a reply, he walked naked into the other room to the wine and the glasses. I usually liked to pull up a sheet at this point and cover myself, but I was too busy watching him. I watched him carefully. Who was on top? Quayle the conqueror—I sensed that he felt triumphant. I would have thought that such triumph would be readable in eye and gesture. Where did he come from? Just what was his real past?

"Here, my dear," Quayle said.

I smiled at him, took the glass.

We did not sip from each other's glass. One of us would have laughed. I kept my face, my eyes as controlled as his. The question was whether he knew. Do the mouse and the cat know which one is which?

"I shall call you within the week," Quayle said.

"And I shall call you," I said.

We smiled again, we nodded, we almost shook hands. I suspected that he already saw me at a desk, a desk in an outer office, an outer office that led to his inner office. In a city that had an apartment, a motel, a suitable *pied à terre*.

I saw him hanging from a rope. Blue eyes bulging from stalks.

Fourteen

The pressures of a life of crime brought on lapses of memory. Who can remember everything? So I bought a bulletin board on which I pinned a list of my due dates, my field notes, those concepts that came to me in moments of clarity. That board was a wilderness of possibilities. Here, for instance, antebellum society in Virginia. There, suggestions for a new economic theory.

That was just the top half of the bulletin board. On the bottom half I posted advertisements for coats, refrigerators, cars, ski lodges. Everything I would buy after the Q payoff.

"Satisfactions," my mother said, "come in different ways. Corruption is elusive."

Once again I considered leaving the city. To Paris? Or the West End of London? Morganstern had said that the blackmailee might talk. What did Morganstern know! Still, if Quayle ever dropped a hint—there I was—an outlaw, an excluded woman, dropped from dinner party lists, maybe admired.

The General sent a second check. I went back to his book. I decided to change the wife.

The General and his wife arrived in Stockholm in the afternoon. The anticipation had almost made him ill. He had taken a window seat and stared at the approaching ground. He had arrived at last. He had hoped somehow that it would be summer—lakes, parks, chains of flowers.

It was cold when they landed, but no wind blew. The General was particularly conscious of the sky. A pure cerulean blue sky. He wore a grey overcoat cut in the slim European fashion. He was not in uniform. The grey coat, his silver hair, the blue sky.

"Nice composition," he told his wife.

"Shall we be private?" she said.

"Private?" he said. "Why would I want to be private? Did I cross the world to be private? Any questions, let me give the answers, unless they catch you alone. You've been briefed, haven't you?"

"Yes," his wife said. "I have my script."

"Remember," the General said, "you adore Sweden, you're honored to be my wife, we live by my philosophy. Got that?"

"Yes," his wife said and clutched her hat.

"And try not to smile so much."

There were many photographers at the airport. He was popular. The photographers really liked him. He wasn't impatient like some of the others. The General let them pose him. He turned this way and that. The General's wife stood and waited. She was thinking about her lover. In the taxi, on the way to the hotel, her husband made her lean back against the cushions. "Don't stick your face against the window," he said. "It makes you look like a match-book girl."

The Committee assigned a guide. They called up from the desk. The General's wife was delighted. She had been alone in the hotel room all day.

The guide came up at once. "My name is Giselle," she said and held out her hand. "I will show you the city and help you through these trying days."

The General's wife clapped her hands. "How nice," she said. "How kind. My husband has been so busy since we arrived. So many interviews. I really didn't know where to go or what to do."

"I'll take care of that," Giselle said. "Concerts, museums, the countryside, shopping. The works."

She stepped back and stared at the General's wife. "While it is on my mind," she said, "what are you wearing for the ceremony? Can you curtsy?"

The General's wife blushed. "I'm uncertain," she said.

139

She opened the closet door. "This," she said and pulled from the rack a yellow crepe dress. "It's new," she said.

Giselle shook her head. "Impossible," she said. She raised the shades for more light. "Why yellow? You are definitely too sallow for that shade."

"My husband likes me in yellow," the General's wife said. "Buy yellow, he said. He approved the selection."

"Won't do," Giselle said and flung the dress across the room, where it collapsed in a quince-colored puddle. "I shall take you shopping. This is my city, and I know the best. Their Royal Highnesses will fall right out of their royal highchairs when they see you."

She was close to tears, the General's wife. "He won't like it," she whispered.

Giselle stood tall, elegant. "That's tough on him. We shall do it anyway," she said. "I see you in black. We'll do you in black satin."

"Oh God," the General's wife said.

"It was marvelous. We saw the Concert Hall. Thiel Gallery, Lidingo—what didn't we see!"

"Where did you get that dress?"

She twirled in front of him. The stiff black satin was cut narrow to show off her figure, her white bosom. Her hair was piled on her head in an intricate arrangement of curls. For jewelry she wore a length of pearls glowing with depth and mystery. They had been borrowed from her guide.

"For the ceremony," she said. "Isn't it wonderful?"

The General looked at her. He thought how people would stare at that white skin, the magnificent curls. "That's the General's wife," they'd say. "Isn't she a knockout?"

"No," he said. "Take it back. I certainly hope that you can take it back. I said yellow, and I meant yellow."

She blushed. Why had she imagined that he would permit her to wear this dress? It was that woman's fault.

She packed the dress in the white box, the pearls in the

140

blue velvet case. It was evening, and she wore her robe. The General watched as she put the box and the case on a chair. He thought about her white skin and the strange arrangement of curls. She had been quite striking. Almost beautiful.

He pushed her down on the bed.

"Now," he said.

"Come to dinner tonight, Harry," I said. There were rumors to be put to sleep. We stood together on the corner by the drug store. It was a chance meeting at two o'clock in the afternoon. Women and children roamed the streets unescorted. Where were the other men?

"I'd like to, babe," Harry said as he shifted his weight from one moccasined foot to the other. "But I have another engagement this evening. Business."

"Sure," I said. In my bag I carried aspirin, talcum, cortisone.

"Got a deal brewing, perking away. Listen, how about tomorrow night?"

Harry was shivering. He wasn't dressed for the cold. "For the cold you have to dress bulky," my mother always said. Harry looked tropical.

"Nice coat," I said. "New?"

"This old thing—don't you remember it? How about tomorrow?"

"All right," I said, "come to dinner tomorrow evening. Bring a picture-puzzle for Leon. He would like one, and it's his turn."

"Sure thing, old girl," Harry said and kissed my cheek. "Taxi," he called out. "Taxi."

I went into Woolworth's and bought a picture-puzzle. No sense leaving everything to chance. When put together, it was a picture of Louis Pasteur stooped over a handful of test tubes.

There was a new poster in the corner of the window of the second-hand bookstore. Or had it been there before?

141

At any event, I wasn't prepared for what I saw. Quayle was lecturing in two days: *Quayle at the New School.* The poster had a white background with black letters. *Eine Leerstelle* was in silver.

I went into the store. I was very fond of that store. "Sammy," I said to the man behind the counter, "do you think that I could get a ticket to the Quayle lecture?"

"Don't know," he said. "Big following, sellout. Maybe for twenty bucks I could arrange something as a favor for a friend."

I gave Sammy a twenty-dollar bill, and he gave me a ticket.

"I asked myself," Harry said, "what will we have to eat—and I answered myself that this feast will be chicken. So the wine is appropriate. Did I guess or did I guess?"

"You guessed," I said. I was crowded at the doorway by the children. Harry had brought wine, Harry had brought two pink roses, Harry had remembered the puzzle.

"Babe Ruth knocking 'em dead," he said and gave Leon his puzzle. Mine was among pots and pans waiting to be slipped into Harry's hands.

Joanne and Richard were smiling.

"She's sure got chicken," Richard said. "Stuffed."

"With wild rice," Leon said.

"The tummy bubbles with joy," Harry said. He gave Richard his black overcoat. Alpaca, I thought.

"It's a good picture of Babe Ruth," Leon said as he looked at the cover of the puzzle box. "I want to be a scientist when I grow up."

"Shut up, kid," Joanne said. "Let's go watch the news."

They moved together towards the living room, a newly bonded group.

"Ballet is an elective at school," Joanne was saying. "I'm thinking about taking it. Mother thinks I should go for carpentry instead. What do you say?"

142

"Any gal with swell legs should go for ballet."

"But I like to make things too. I just don't know."

The voices were lost in the sounds of the world. That evening's world. I opened the oven door and watched the crisply glowing bird.

Harry came back. "Want a drink?"

"Yes," I said. "A Scotch."

"Sure," Harry said and poured into two glasses. "Remember Ackman?"

"No."

"You do," Harry said. "Thin man, very thin man. He's tall."

"Maybe," I said.

"You do. He just took out a patent. A sweet patent—something to do with tractors."

"Tractors? In New York?"

"He thought it through, you see. He's into gadgets. He's going out to Iowa and open a plant."

"A plant in Iowa."

"Ackman's dream. The thing is, May, I'm going with him."

I turned to get a good look at him.

"Money?"

"I don't need a dime, May. Not a dime. Ackman's wife came into some. I'm going to be like a managing director."

"All right, Harry."

"Do you think I should tell the kids?"

"About what?"

"About Iowa. I mean it will be hard on them—not that Iowa is the end of the world. There are planes. I'll work up to it. I'll tell them later."

"Right," I said. "Carry this to the table."

The dinner was a success. There was chicken stuffed with wild rice, there were fresh baby peas in a delicate butter sauce, and my super endive salad with Aunt Giselle's secret dressing. There was pie.

"I've decided to go with woodworking," Joanne said. "Freak those jocks out. Anyway, I'm good at making things."

"Fine decision," Harry said.

"Anyway," Joanne said, "I'm too old to begin ballet."

"You'd look stupid," Richard said. "Waving your arms around."

"Eat," I ordered.

All in all, the evening wasn't bad. They left the kitchen. They left me with dishes. Everyone was polite.

Afterwards, Joanne took Leon to the library. It was a special treat in honor of Harry. Richard and Harry went back to the living room.

"Sports," Harry said. "Sports are important, Richard."

"If I got sick," Richard said, "would you take care of me?"

"Of course. What a question! Your old dad would take care of you."

"How'd I find you?" Richard said. "I never know exactly where you are. You move around."

"A man's got to be on the move," Harry said, "to make a living, son. But no matter, I would take care of you when you got sick."

"How'd you know if I was sick? I mean where would I call?"

"I'd know. Dad would know."

"I could call Mom," Richard said, "even if she wasn't here. She writes stuff on her calendar. I could call Grace or Huldie or Rosemary. Grace's a pain. Joanne is a pain too, but she'd take care of me if I got sick. She'd take care of me if I got sick, and Mom was dead. I'd take care of Leon. I beat up kids if they bother him. I do it all the time. I'd take care of Leon, and Joanne would take care of me or Grace or Huldie would."

"I'd take care of you," Harry said. "Honest, son, I would."

The phone rang. "I'll get it," I called out. "I'll get it."

It was the General.

"I got the stuff," he said. "Picked it up today." We were using a mail drop. "I liked it," the General continued. "I mean I really liked it."

"Good," I said. "Fine."

"The confession," the General said. "Just what I had in mind, the entangled legs, the peach."

"All right," I said.

"It's the other stuff," the General said. "I thought maybe there had been a mistake. Pages shifted, misprinted, happens all the time here. I mean I can't see what you have in mind—no criticism meant, you understand—but that trip to Sweden? Was that supposed to be in my book?"

I didn't hesitate. "No," I said. "Pages shifted, Just discard that section."

"I'll have it shredded," the General said. "Would you like to have a catalogue of sexual devices? I happen to have a copy. Swell ideas."

"No," I said.

I went into my alcove. Sometimes I made changes. Sometimes I practiced diplomacy. So I removed some papers from the General's file. The alterations could be made. The pages held for another time.

For a start I switched the first line.

C.R. and his wife arrived in Stockholm in the afternoon, I wrote.

I thought about a later insertion. That I put on a separate piece of paper. Insertion A, I called it.

Insertion A: Nobel wished that he had packed ear plugs. The sounds of people around him seemed to reverberate in his very spine. He should have taken a private train car, never mind that the journey was short. He felt the pressure of people, they jostled him. He couldn't even stand their touch. Why didn't they all go somewhere? Wasn't there some place for them all?

Fifteen

"I'm practical," Quayle said, holding the receiver very close to his mouth. "You'll find me practical. The salary will be more than adequate. I don't know about moving expenses. The university wouldn't normally pay moving expenses at your level. But never mind, my dear. We shall manage."

"Manage," I said.

"Basically," Quayle said, "the job will be cushy. There's storage in the anteroom that I have in mind for you, but I'll have that all moved out and a fresh coat of paint. You'll like that, won't you? Then we'll let you pick the furniture, May. Something that blends with mine. I've got distressed oak. I see chrome for you. Chrome and black. But the choice will be yours. Any questions?"

"Chippendale."

"What?"

"Chippendale."

"You mean for the furniture? In your office?"

"And don't think that you can pass off any imitations from North Carolina," I said. "I want the chairs with pierced splats. Tables in the *rocaille* style. Look for quality gilding, inlay."

"They would never pay for that, May. How could you expect them to pay for that? And what about my office—I would have to change everything in my office too."

"Yes," I said.

There was a pause. "I've thought it through," Quayle said. "We don't have to decide this matter now. We'll negotiate it later—perhaps one piece at a time. Furniture after all is furniture.

"Now about living arrangements," Quayle said. "There's an apartment that's come free in a building owned by a friend of mine. Not the suburbs here, but then the suburbs are a touch Nosey Parker, if you get my

146

meaning. But my friend assures me that the apartment is sunny, three bedrooms. Two of your children would have to double up."

"I've got four bedrooms now," I said.

"Three is the best I could do," Quayle's voice exploded with annoyance. "Three! What's a room more or less? The street is safe, trees, a few. Schools."

"Mother," Joanne said, "aren't you ever going to get off the phone? I told you that *someone* might call me. Why don't we get another phone? Another number?"

"She never used to be on the phone so much. Not evenings anyway," Richard said. "Who's she talk to?"

"Who cares?" Joanne said. "She's in love with some creep maybe. A new daddy-oh."

"Harry's our daddy," Leon said. "We don't need two of them."

"I hear voices," Quayle said. "I distinctly hear voices. Who's there?"

"People," I said.

"Safe? May, is this call safe?"

"Yes," I said.

"Try to be here by the first of next month," Quayle said. "They like people to start on the first. It makes for uncomplicated bookkeeping. Here's the address. Get a pencil, May, and write this down. You can ship directly to the apartment."

It's amazing what people will ask you to do.

"I've got a pencil," I said. "I've got a number two pencil and paper, plenty of paper. Taking pencil in hand, Quayle, I write a word. Want to know the word? The word is money."

"*Money?*"

"Money."

"We have an agreement," Quayle said.

I wondered if he was making a fist, fingernails digging into the palm. Didn't I hear voices just past the range of the receiver? The bastard had people too.

147

The lady in yellow and just a few friends in for another celebration. All so glad to know him. Chilled martinis, ancient Scotch. All sitting on foam rubber cushions. "How does he do it?" someone says. "The man's organized, that's how," someone says. Someone laughs. "I believe that he knows everyone, all the great minds of the age. Prudhomme, Dunant, Röntgen, Zeeman, van't Hoff, Fischer, von Behring, Ross Mommsen, Lorentz, Passy, Ducommun, Gobat, Becquerel, Curie, Curie, Finsen, Björnson, Mistral, Cremer, von Suttner, Lenard, Thomson, Pavlov, Koch, Eizaguirre, Kipling."

"Quayle," I said. Could he hear me with all that noise? I took a chance. "Quayle, deliver the money to me by Saturday—or if I were you, I'd cancel my trip to Sweden."

"May, I can't believe this. How can you say that? How? Are you heartless?" he said. "After what happened between us, what we've been to each other. I liked you, May."

"Mother," Joanne said, "it simply isn't fair. It's filthy rotten, that's what. Hang up that phone!"

"Who's she talking to?" Richard said.

"I like Harry," Leon said.

I calmed my voice. Quayle must have closed a door, all those sounds had departed. "I have prepared," I lied, "have typed, and proofread a document for delivery to all major newspapers. Twenty-six papers just on the East Coast—not to speak of the wire services."

"You haven't!"

"I have connections," I lied.

"What about our plans?" he said. "We were going to be together. What about that?"

"Money," I said.

"My life has lost direction," Quayle said. "When I am relaxed on those quiet mornings when I can sit alone at the table with my coffee, I say to myself that this is not going to happen. I say to myself who will believe her."

"I could name ten," I said. "As stated in chapter three

of *Eine Leerstelle*, the need for self-deception makes monkeys out of us all."

Sixteen

Clumps of people clung to the doorway, to the bolted doors. Boys in heavy plaid shirts put their arms around their girls. All the girls were small next to the boys in the plaid shirts. The boys held them away from the crowd. There were middle-aged women and men wearing gold chains. I wanted a seat in the back. Suppose I didn't like the lecture. I mean can you sneak out from the second row?

"I heard him speak," someone said. "I was in Cleveland in spring visiting my sister, and I heard him speak." She wasn't young, and two young girls turned to stare at her with disdain.

"Understanding," one of the girls said, unbuttoning her leather coat. The other girl nodded. It was all code.

I was careful not to say anything. Better not to say anything. Wasn't the purpose of a lecture to listen? "Quit shoving," someone said. The doors were unbolted, and the waves of soft bodies swept me onward.

"Does he autograph?" a man asked me.

"No," I said.

"Sit together?"

"No," I said.

I pushed forward to find what I wanted, a seat in the middle of the last row. I removed my raincoat, folded it across my lap. There was an excitement about the evening, the intenseness of the audience. Most of those around me had copies of the book. The woman who sat next to me, for instance.

"Why bring the book?" I asked.

She didn't want to talk to me. Her face was puffy, perhaps from tears. She pulled her elbow away from the narrow chair arm that separated us. "I don't share *my* book," she said.

"That's all right." I was cheerful. "I don't want a share, but what do you do with it?"

"You don't follow, do you?"

"I guess not," I said.

"When he reads, I follow," she said.

"He reads?"

"He's going to read."

"He's going to read from *Eine Leerstelle*?"

"Certainly. What are you here for anyway?"

I was disappointed. A lecture is a lecture. I wanted slides, rounded hills, other strata.

The woman next to me looked around, but the auditorium was full, there were no empty seats. She half-turned in her seat, facing the opposite direction. I looked at the man seated on the other side of me. He was accompanied by a woman who wore a cloak with a hood that concealed her face. He said words like "opportunistic," "diseased," "draconian," and possibly, "insight."

I looked at my watch. It was definitely time for the lecture to begin. I wished that I had brought a book, I wanted something to read, to pass the time there among the unfriendly.

This was not your typical audience. Here we were already late. Was this audience impatient? Where were the stamping feet? The catcalls? The cries of "Bring on the dancing girls!" No, this was a docile, even a subdued audience. And didn't I hear that many had heard him speak before? Didn't someone say four times? Travelled to different cities to hear him.

He was a hit. I just hadn't realized what a hit he was. I observed how the young girls leaned forward in their seats, angled their bodies forward in anticipation. He was coming. Any minute now.

"When surrounded by many people," my mother said, "watch for trouble."

"Try," Aunt Giselle said, "to keep it down to three."

I was aware of crowd conduct. You do different things in a crowd. I joined the crowd. Now I too was subdued, now I too leaned forward at the waist. We all went— "Aah!"—when the lights dimmed. Then the music started. I was surprised. I looked at my neighbors. They weren't surprised. I did not approve.

What was the matter with Quayle? The addition of music was not appropriate. It definitely showed no understanding of *Eine Leerstelle*, a lack of taste. It ruined my mood. I leaned back in my chair. *Ba, ba, bop. Ba, ba, bop.* The sound was quadraphonic. It got louder, picked up a jazz beat. Oh Quayle, for shame!

I was afraid of being stoned as I tripped over feet or I would have left the auditorium. I waited for a drum roll. There was a drum roll.

The music roared to an end. Now this became a very silent room, no shuffling feet, no echoing whispers, no frightened coughs. Was I the only newcomer in the auditorium? All the bodies around me seemed to know what would happen. The single light on the stage, a high stool, a folding table, the glass of water. That was good. It was a glass of water, no paper cup.

Quayle entered from the right, a slow easy walk. He wore a loose grey sweater and grey slacks, no tie, no coat. Now there was a sigh of contentment, almost a chant. I entered again into the crowd spirit. I sighed.

Quayle knew exactly what to do. I marveled at that. He moved the stool forward, found that unsatisfactory and moved it back. Fine touch. The audience waited. He sipped from the glass. He pulled at both pants legs and climbed upon the stool.

He shook a copy of *Eine Leerstelle* from his back

151

pocket. I knew the cover. That was not the real cover. Either Quayle had it specially made or it was encased in some plastic. Was he trying for special effects?

The book glowed with silvery light. Terrible for people wearing glasses. I considered it too bright, too tacky. Better to have the book minus the cover. Better not to detract from the book.

"*Eine Leerstelle,*" Quayle said.

"*Eine Leerstelle,*" said the audience.

Me too.

Quayle had a microphone clipped to his sweater, his voice never whistled. It was a rehearsed voice, modulated, with a successful use of highs and lows.

"We begin," Quayle said.

No one contradicted him.

"The mood that I am in," Quayle said, "is a solemn one. A solemn one placed on me by the honor that I have been given. I know that you are all aware of the honor that I have been given. It humbles me." Quayle paused. "But," he said, "it does not humble *Eine Leerstelle*. No, it does not humble the book at all. In this mood, I shall do chapter five. I feel that chapter five best expresses the mood.

"As usual at intermission break, you may make requests. I will randomly select one request."

"What does that mean?" I chanced a whisper to the half-turned woman.

She glared. "You give a request to the usher, they go into a bowl, and he picks one."

"Wow," I said and opened my purse to find a pen and my small pad. "On any kind of paper?"

"Hush," the woman said. "You are destroying my concentration, my mood, the orbit of my planet. Any type of paper. What does that matter? It's the thought."

I had to be certain as Jupiter skirted Mars. "Just pick a chapter?"

"Yes! For God's sake, just pick a chapter. He especially likes chapters one and eight."

152

I'll bet he did. I could see him really putting himself into those. Sighs, wiping the eyes, rolling the *r*'s. This would be my choice though, one I picked to stock the bowl with my own kind of fish. In the dim light I began to rip pages from my note pad. On each sheet of paper I wrote the number three. No attempts to conceal my handwriting. A bunch of three's.

I had the papers all ready. No one was paying attention to what I was doing. They were all listening to Quayle. I didn't feel that was necessary. I knew chapter five. Chapter five did not express my mood.

I wondered if they would let me drop all these pieces of paper into the bowl. Some were folded, some were not. Perhaps I might palm some of them, permitting them to slip from my fingers into the bowl.

I couldn't stand the wait until intermission. Chapter five was long. Quayle dragged it out too, pauses, stares into space. I controlled my need for restless movements such as I made in movies. So often someone would touch my shoulder. "Sit still," they'd say. "Can't you sit still?"

It was over. There was a moment of sharp silence, and then everyone applauded. I applauded too and listened for catcalls or whistles or stamping feet. They only applauded.

With not a backward look nor acknowledgement of the audience, Quayle left the stage.

The lights came on, we blinked, and people began to move into the aisles. The woman next to me said, "Excuse me." She squeezed past.

"Wait," I called. "When does the usher come?"

"Come? He comes. It doesn't matter. I told you it's always one and eight."

"Maybe," I said. "Times change, though." I didn't think that the woman heard me, because she hurried into the line of people moving slowly outward.

I stood up, breathed deeply, stretched. Most of the audience was young, having a good time. They looked pleased, relaxed. The evening was what they had expected. But it wasn't a lecture as billed.

I almost missed that usher. He didn't call out. He was quiet, disaffected. He carried a small glass fish bowl that already held a layer of pieces of paper. White sheets, torn bits, yellow foolscap, blue note cards.

"Here, here," I said and made my way to the aisle. Everyone between my seat and the aisle had left. I was embarrassed by my fistful of paper. "I've got everyone's here," I said. 'All my friends have made their choices." I didn't have to bother. What did he care. He only held the bowl. I unloaded my choice. The job, I assumed, was just for the evening. He did not look well. He looked cold and tired.

"I hope I'm lucky," I said.

"Yeah," the usher said and moved away.

I went back to my seat prepared to wait. How was it with these readers? Was the lecture a success? The audience returned. It was then that I could tell how things stood. I watched for empty seats, for suddenly remembered errands, for the results of quickly made liaisons. Only one empty seat. In my section.

Quayle followed the same routine, appearing in a moment of suspense. He wore a navy sweater and matching slacks. I turned to the women next to me. "Costume change?"

The movement of her body suggested the depth of her disapproval. "He sweats," she said. "It's exhausting."

Quayle perched on his stool. "*Eine Leerstelle*," he said, "offers choices. May I have the bowl of selections?"

The usher, looking more weary and shivering on the stage, brought him the bowl. It was filled now with paper but not tightly packed. I couldn't calculate whether the odds were in my favor.

Quayle stared at the audience. "May I have a volunteer," he said, "to pick out our choice for the evening?"

They were all going along with it. That's the crowd

thing. Me—I would have liked one inappropriate giggle, I prayed for an inappropriate giggle. For two children to nudge each other and say, "Hey, you go, not me." Quayle pointed. He must have decided who would do it from the offering hands. I didn't count how many had volunteered.

A young girl got up from her seat in the second or third row and pushed past people to get to the stage. She wore jeans and a loose white sweater. Her hair hung long and free. Who was she? Her face was revealed when she stood next to Quayle. Even from where I sat I could see how her eyes were glowing, her expression neither sullen nor tired. The color in her cheeks was the result of embarrassment, excitement, pleasure.

I leaned forward in my seat. What was the scent? What did they spray through the ventilating system? There was the smell of a tropical perfume, oleander and a touch of wild fern. It made my nose itch.

But still my attention was firm. I watched that girl as a mother watches her child. Wait a minute—that was my child!

"Young lady," Quayle said in a tone of voice that I could have predicted. "Will you do me the honor of picking our next selection?"

"Sure," Joanne said, her voice made hoarse perhaps by the acoustical system. "I mean yes."

"Very well. The bowl, please."

Joanne's hand dipped into the bowl, fumbled, her fingers closed over a fold of paper. She held it out to Quayle.

"No, no," he said. "You read it."

"Three," Joanne read. She could have been an actress, her voice carried so well.

"Three?"

"Three."

"Well, thank you. Thank you, young lady."

Joanne smiled, a slight ducking of the head, and marched off the stage. I was proud of her. Nepotism notwithstanding.

Look at Quayle! Quayle was squirming on his stool like some trapped schoolboy who hadn't spat on his palms fast enough. He coughed. The sonorous voice had lost its pitch. In a moment he would claim a cold.

I looked at my neighbors in the audience. Some looked uneasy. "He never read three before," someone whispered. "I prefer eight myself," someone said.

"Poor man," the woman next to me said. "He is truly worn."

"Chapter three," I said, "is very hard on the nerves."

"I hardly ever read that one," the woman said, suddenly convivial. "I wonder who did it to him."

Me.

I did it, I wanted to say. My arm suddenly throbbed to life, the ache sharp and piercing. My sleeve was moist. I needed to go home and bathe the wound. I bent my arm, holding it close to the warmth of my body.

Quayle once again opened his copy of *Eine Leerstelle*. He did the clothing adjustment, the stool jiggle. I saw his fingers fumble with the book. Possibly he sought the index, possibly he had to find chapter three.

I wanted to ask Joanne, "Which chapter do you like best?"

"Chapter of what?" she'd ask.

"*Eine Leerstelle*."

"How did you know I read *Eine Leerstelle*?"

I wouldn't answer that. "Try chapter three," I'd say.

Quayle cleared his throat with peccary grunts.

The house lights dimmed.

"Oh God," he moaned.

Now *that* I heard.

"*In the beginning*," he read, "*Giselle and Sonya were told . . .*"

Seventeen

I found during this period that I was having a hard time making conversation, bothered as I was both by *tranquillitas* and *apatheia*. There were subjects spoken about on the telephone and in person. For instance, there was the subject of Huldie's marriage. There was also C.R. and Giselle stuck in a backwater of California. And there was a persistent woman from an historically important group who came to my door one day insisting upon employing me.

She arrived at the point when I had C.R. and Giselle driving through California—a listing of streets, towns, names of motels. It was an American experience—a newsreel. They had rented a pink stucco-covered house built on a concrete slab without a cellar. They thought about working, regular jobs, maybe in the movie industry.

"Do you think that he'll find us?" C.R. said.

"Perhaps," Giselle said.

"God," C.R. said. *"I never intended this. What will we do?"*

"One thing," Giselle said, *"one thing is true. If Nobel comes here, there's no place to hide—one lousy floor."*

I left my alcove to go to the door.

"You can't get away," the woman said, swooping down like the bird of darkness. She had kept the doorbell going, but even so, she looked respectable.

"I told you on the phone," I said. "No more assignments until after the first of the year. I'm all booked, booked solid."

I was not in a businesslike mood. The vial from Sweden had just arrived that morning. "An experimental drug," Dr. Miller from the building next door had said, "not yet approved by the FDA." The shot hurt, my arm hurt.

"I am destroyed," the woman said. She had trouble finding a handkerchief. "I promised them," she wept. She became at once a crumpled figure. "It's for the Two Hundredth Anniversary."

Had I invited this woman in? She was in my living room anyway. She had been with me nearly a half-hour. First she had cajoled, then threatened. She had been imperious. "Do you know who I *know*?" she had demanded.

"All right, all right," I said at last. I was rude. "Don't think that you can come near me. though. When it is finished, it is finished."

"On time?"

"On time," I said. I looked into her pale eyes. "Sign the check," I said.

"We are," she said, "the oldest. The very oldest."

"Right," I said. I closed the door behind her.

The telephone rang. "No," I said. "Not now."

When the telephone rang again, I turned on the answering machine. Let him talk to that!

I was going to give myself some free time. Anyway, I was weary from meditating. Tired of the sense of intimate violation, knowing just how sweaty my hands would be.

Joanne brought home a strange object made of wood. "Here," she said. "For you."

"Swell," I said. It was beautiful, carefully rubbed and held together by wooden screws. The wood was pecan.

"Don't pretend," Joanne said, "that you know what it's for."

"No," I said, turning it over in my hands. It was heavy. "I haven't the slightest idea."

"It's an arm rest that attaches to the arm of a chair and further elevates the limb. I found a picture of it in a seventeenth-century book of household items. A physician's limb raiser, it was called. So I copied it. I measured the arm of that chair in your office. It fits. You can rest your sore arm on it from time to time if you want."

"My God but it's beautiful," I said. There was no note of false compliment in my voice. "It's a real work of art."

"I knew she'd like it," Leon said. He turned to Richard. "You said it was weird."

Richard said, "Shut up or I'll break both your legs."

I went into my alcove. The arm rest fitted perfectly on the arm of my chair. My arm slid into the carved canal.

So I took a break. I sat in my alcove, resting my arm, sipping coffee. But Quayle clung to the battlements of my mind. Quayle marching on the pages of history carrying the banner of my efforts. Quayle on the Dick Cavett Show. My mother always said, "If they take something from you, they run with it."

That was it then, he had taken *Eine Leerstelle*—my act of creation, my balloon, my kite.

"Think about civil disobedience," my mother always advised. "If they get you, be certain that it's worth it."

"It's how you view the Self that counts," Aunt Giselle said.

"Hit the *gonifs* where they breathe," my mother said.

"Heart," Aunt Giselle said.

I definitely wasn't asking for enough. I was going to raise the ante.

"Messages," Joanne called. "You left the abominable machine on. A Q wants to talk to you—is that Q as in Don Q? Grace said speak to you tomorrow. The poet said call back."

"All right," I said. "Thank you."

Richard came into the alcove. "Look what was in the piano bench," he said. Richard had found the travel brochures. There was quite a collection, some sent for, some taken from travel agents by pretending to be a traveller.

"Are we going somewhere?"

"Perhaps."

"We never go anywhere."

"Never mind," I said. "Lands seldom look like those pictures anyway. They photograph them from strange angles, increase the size, deepen the colors."

"Can I go to the movies tonight?" Richard said.

"No," I said.

I dialed my first number.

"He's not here," the secretary said. She sounded tired now, anxious. Had she heard rumors that he was bringing in someone new? Quayle was always looking for someone new.

"Have him call me, please," I said. "Tell him May called."

"Yes," the woman said. She didn't ask for a number.

I knew what she thought.

What did she care if he was fooling around. Famous men always did. Probably had an apartment somewhere.

The poet was in, though.

"Sweets," Peter said. "I have been waiting. Waiting. I have verse for you, May. I want you to hear it first."

I closed my eyes. "Not today, Peter. Not today."

"It's dedicated to you, May. *To May.*"

That's how I was trapped—caught by good manners and gratitude. "All right," I said. "But I have to start dinner soon."

"Lean back. sweets. Relax. I based these, you know, on what's happened to you recently—like an inspiration." He coughed. "No titles." He coughed again.

"Dwarfs—small men—lovers of different kinds
Each time she appeared
Each occurrence out of time
We walked, my love and I down the rue de Campine
See, my love said. That woman again
Giselle speaking a Siren's song with dark berry lips
To someone with face unseen
I saw her first as a butterfly
I recognized in myself I preferred
Such a simple view, such a short season
It's easy to love children."

"Peter," I said.

"Wait, sweets," he said. "Listen to this.

160

"There are cases of extreme mutilation
On this floor   Where a former lover is
Good of you to come   Giselle says
The other floors were over-utilized
They put me here   Close your eyes
In the halls   There are half-people
Here   There are rounded, taped
Edges   Fear to look down there
Avoid direct questions about function
Soon, I'll leave   Giselle says   They are
Almost through with me. She is a former lover
Seen clearly in this place   Under control
I close my eyes down the hall   Past
Rounded, taped edges   Where no one can beckon"

"Peter," I said.

"Yes, sweets."

"The poems?"

"Published."

"Already?"

"Yes."

We ate early. You tend to eat early when you eat with children. I made spaghetti alla carbonara, garlic bread, and a romaine and onion salad.

"Your arm looks blue," Joanne said. "Why blue?"

"It's from the new shot," I said. "The shot did it."

"How sick are you?" Richard said.

"Fine," I said. "I feel fine. But I have more work to do tonight—so I want volunteers for the dishes."

"Who?"

"All of you," I said.

Quayle did not eat early.

"This call," Quayle said, "is disrupting my dinner party."

"I've been thinking," I said. "I've been reflecting. *Eine Leerstelle*, according to *Publishers Weekly*, is in its twenty-fifth printing—so many, many copies."

"What are you up to?" Quayle said. "I will not tolerate this."

"More," I said. "The rates are going up."

"What?" Quayle was shouting into the phone.

"A change in the monthly stipend, the honorarium, my lifetime cash flow. One thousand a month," I said.

"Robbery!" he said. "This scheme won't work, May Alto. You can go just so far. Do you think that my supply of money is endless? Suspicions will arise."

"One thousand," I said. "Each month, every month. First payment due now. Second, the day you return."

"I know what you are thinking," Quayle said. "You think that after I have received the prize the fear of scandal will be greater and you'll raise the sum again. Think again, my girl. This is no child that you are dealing with."

I hung up.

I had only twenty-four hours to Morganstern. I would meditate some more, give the entire evening over to meditation.

But if I hurried I could make some notes, fit them in later. I took the folder of my newest client. Two Hundredth Anniversary was the label. The woman had supplied a bibliography about the founder, the life of the founder. I headed a page—"Before the Founding."

A Poet Laureate was at the house one evening. They took in transients. Times were bad. "Make room," the mother always said. The founder at that time was a bone-thin child. The family lived in a house thirty blocks from Lake Michigan. The house was also five blocks from a brewery. At two in the morning a crudely made, relatively ineffective bomb went off at the brewery. Basically, the work of amateurs. It was August. The flying bricks smashed all the blue glass windows in a building that held the vats. No one at the founder's house claimed knowledge of the act. The Poet Laureate slept upstairs. In the kitchen until well past

162

four o'clock the mother sat and spoke to Beatrice Webb. There were witnesses. The child learned in school that Lake Michigan was one of the Great Lakes.

Another time they lived in a house with asbestos siding and a roof with a terrific slant. The house was less than two miles from Lake Michigan. The house was also fifteen blocks from another brewery. One night at ten past midnight, a bomb went off at the brewery, intoxicating the air for miles. Two men with credentials came to the house to get the child's mother. The child kicked one of the men shin-high. He reached out to grab the child, but the mother caught his wrist. His grey fedora hat fell off. Like to broke it, he said later. The child learned in school all about shipping on the Great Lakes, with particular emphasis on Lake Michigan. At no time, however, did the child ever dip toes in that icy refreshing water. Not for one single hot summer day. Children remember things like that.

Eighteen

Coming up was my last session with Morganstern. I served for breakfast waffles, real maple syrup, and tiny sausage links. I was hungry. My horoscope in yesterday's newspaper had predicted crossing planets.

"It looks like a Sunday breakfast," Richard said as he sat down.

"How are we supposed to eat all this?" Joanne warned. "We are not going to be late."

"I like my sausages with fennel," Leon said.

"Eat as much as you want," I offered.

Joanne looked at me. "Some of my friends—Sandra, Bobby, Tish—are going up to Lake George for Saturday and Sunday."

"No," I said. Should I wear my black slacks again? A suit?

"How young do you think I am?" Joanne said.

"Sixteen," I said.

I moved plates. Richard was saying something about playing in a game. Something about not wanting to play in a game. Joanne said that everyone she knew was planning to leave home as soon as possible.

I decided at that moment to go again in black. That was how he saw me. Would Morganstern be pleased with my progress? I hoped so. After all, I had sat in my alcove, I had sat on the couch, twice I tried sitting by the kitchen table—I was meditating everywhere. Three times I erased the dark waters of the womb.

The doorbell sounded.

"Who the hell is here this early?" Joanne said. She stood up. We all stood up.

It was Grace. Grace dressed for the office, for the job. "Hi, kids," she said. "I must see you, May. I cannot sleep—I am exhausted. But I have just a moment."

Joanne nodded. The children wearing their knapsacks left the battlefield of the kitchen.

"What is it, Grace?" I said. "Coffee? Waffles?"

"One moment," Grace said. "I have only one moment."

I looked at her closely. She was wearing large dark glasses. I thought that the skin around one eye might be bruised.

"We must stop her," Grace said. "We are her friends. We must stand by her."

"Who?" I said.

"Huldie," Grace said. "For God's sakes, it's Huldie. How can she marry this man? I met him. He lacks sensibilities. He lacks fervor. He's from out of town."

"I wouldn't think of stopping her," I said.

Wasn't it Grace who had lent me a dress—a lipstick? "Be seductive," she advised. "It's a real-life romance."

164

"You heard it here first," Aunt Giselle said.

There had been a blue convertible.

"What I want to know," Mother had said, "is do you have to get married—the whole thing can be arranged, you see."

Grace paced, fidgeted, nibbled on a waffle, sugar coated her finger. She looked at her watch. "Four minutes," she said, "on the meter. Hers doesn't like me to be late."

"We can't stop Huldie," I said.

"Why?"

"Risky," I said. "Real risky."

I washed, put on my black slacks, black sweater, no makeup. He'd recognize me. When the phone rang, I was thinking Quayle. I had gone that far in meditation.

"I'm through being a nice guy," Quayle said. "I want you to understand that. My wife is at home packing for the eventful trip. I have received copies of the final itinerary. Afterwards, there will be a European tour. They want to hear me everywhere. Nothing, nothing shall stop me."

"Maybe," I said.

"May Alto," Quayle said. He was breathing into the telephone. "Do you know what can be done with twenty-five thousand dollars? There's a lot you can do with a sum like that. A lot, May Alto. I have excellent investment counselors. We'll help you."

"All," I said.

"Wait," he ordered, but I was already replacing the receiver.

Huldie would know that Grace had been to see me. No astrologer's signals, no tea leaves. Grace would simply tell her. And in the last hour of my meditation, Huldie came to the apartment. Huldie is small, almost tiny.

"I've called in sick," she said. "Feel terrible about doing that."

I offered coffee. The waffles were gone.

"Oh, nothing," Huldie said and sat down. "On the fifteenth," she said, "I'm going to be married. It's all settled. I've made the arrangements. And I don't care, I want three matrons of honor. I want the three of you."

Huldie looked almost shy, the way she kept biting her lips. And I remembered when we had stood together, for instance, the time when the man in the fedora hat came.

"I'd be honored," I said. "Where will the wedding be?"

"In my apartment," Huldie said. "I'm waiting."

"Waiting for what?"

"Aren't you going to say that this is too sudden? Everyone else has. Come to your senses, they say. Think of the children, they say. Aren't you going to ask if I know him well enough? Think about the last time, they say. Didn't you swear never again?

"May, you remember my husband? One husband. He went after an actress. I never really said before, but he did. Older than me—but there was the reputation. You know what you can do when your husband goes after an actress—nothing. Grace says that I'm crazy."

I hadn't intended to say anything that Grace had said. I wasn't going to mention Grace at all. "Listen," I said, "be happy. Are you going to live in Minnesota?"

Huldie nodded. "Yes," she said. "It's a change. A change for me, a change for the kids."

"Change is good," I said. "Or at least it can be. Don't knock change."

"We can always come back," Huldie said. "I told the kids that. I'm subletting the apartment. I gave two weeks' notice at my office, but I said that I know someone. Actually, I said that I may know someone. There are good benefits, May. There's a great deal of security, and the work is decently proportioned. You'd fit in. You'd like it."

I looked at my watch. "I have to get across town," I said. "I have an appointment."

"Think about it, May."

"I will."

Huldie looked down at her lap, plucked at threads. "His family used to own a kind of boardinghouse," she said. "My mother stayed there once, and your mother. They all went to California together, then they came back. Now she lives there, his mother. She puts henna on her hair, he says. She belongs to some group and sends him letters about dark forces."

"Don't worry," I said and patted her hand. "She probably won't ever come back twice. They seldom do."

Nineteen

Morganstern's inner sanctum was in disarray. He had buzzed me into the waiting room and left me stranded there. When I marched into his office, I found him sitting Indian-fashion on the floor. His tweed jacket hung from the doorknob, and his necktie was draped over the back of a chair. There was a considerable amount of debris on the floor. Piles of papers fanned out from stacks of books.

"I'm taking an inventory," Morganstern said. "I cancelled all my appointments except yours." He motioned in the direction of a chair.

"I had sex with him," I said, and sat down.

Morganstern unfolded one leg and an entire fan of papers blew outward. "I want you to look at this list I've made," he said. "It's here somewhere."

"Sex," I said. "With him."

"You?" Morganstern said, momentarily. "Who with?"

"The client." I looked down at Morganstern.

"The blackmailee?"

"Him," I said.

Morganstern moved as if to rise and then fell back. "I see," he said. "You had a meeting with him. Was force employed?"

"You mean did he hold me down? Not exactly."

"Does this mean that you will abandon the plan?"

"Are you kidding?" My resolve was steel. Couldn't he see that?

"Did you meditate?" Morganstern said. "Did you sit quietly and think about the consequences of this behavior, about the stresses of your life, about what a life of crime will mean to your family? There are children?"

"Three."

"Suppose you are incarcerated?"

"Jailed."

"Jailed. What then? What will happen to your children when this man turns you in to the police?"

"Morganstern," I said, "you worry too much."

"You mean you don't believe that he will. You think victims don't turn on their victimizers. That's what you think? Can he afford what you are asking?"

"Yes," I said. "He can afford."

"Good," Morganstern said. "Now, did you do it?"

"It?"

"The meditation. What was your program?"

"I sought spiritual intuition. A sense of unity, a sense of purpose."

"No good," Morganstern said. "You should have envisioned yourself in prison greys. You should have seen your children bereft, taunted by schoolmates, abandoned. The savagery of society."

"Soap opera," I said.

"Have you ever," Morganstern said, "thought of doing something else?"

"Not blackmail?"

"A job—a different way of earning a living. Have you ever thought being all these different people may be causing you pain that you are unwilling to recognize?"

If you had a real job, some place to go.

"Also," Morganstern said, "we should move backwards. Back to the start of it."

"It?"

"Blackmail."

"Two and one-half weeks?"

Morganstern stamped the side of his heel on the floor. "What good is that? We know what happened for two and one-half weeks—demands for money, fucking, meditation. You have to go farther back."

"The blackmail is new, the request for money is brand-new."

"Bull," Morganstern said. "The beginning, May. It all goes back to the beginning. Explore. Exploration is everything. When did you meet him?"

"Seven years ago."

"Seven," Morganstern said. "That's a solid number—that's a number with biblical significance." He looked away. "Who is he?" he snapped.

Now that was good, authoritative. I could have raised my hand and given the answer. But shadows of Quayle, shades of Quayle were grouped around Morganstern. I had no intention of invoking his presence for Morganstern. Better that Morganstern shouldn't know.

"Almost caught me that time," I said.

Morganstern kicked a book. "Back," he said. "Back farther. I've changed my mind—start back."

"Can't do that," I said. "I'm not the same person. I am essentially different. I believe that as time passes we become different persons."

"Same," Morganstern said. "The evolving-personality theory."

"Different person," I said. "Like I was someone else. For instance, seven years ago I was someone's wife. Not only am I no longer someone's wife, but I am not certain whether I can remember exactly what it was like to be a wife. Different person."

"That's it," Morganstern said. "You had an affair—seven years ago with the blackmailee."

"No," I said. "Not me."

"I ought to stand up," Morganstern said.

"Don't bother," I said. "If you're comfortable, I don't mind."

"Thank you," he said. He coughed. "Let us return to your problem. To begin with, it's a real crime."

"My mother used to say fear gets nothing done."

"He'll tell," Morganstern said. "For a lot of money, he'll tell. Nothing is a scandal anymore. Do you think that anything is a scandal today?"

I nodded my head. "It's because of what you hear," I said. "As a receiver of confessions, you have a distorted view. You think that everything does. It doesn't. Some facts are never revealed."

"My God, May," Morganstern whispered, "what do you have on this man?"

He looked down, rubbed his hair. He saw something and slapped his hand on the floor. "Here," he said. "Here it is. Didn't I tell you it was here? My list." He offered me the paper, and I bent over to take it.

"Books," I said. "Four hundred and fifty-two books."

"My personal library," Morganstern said proudly. "It took me most of the day to get them down. I have book shelves in my living room next door, floor to ceiling. I've emptied them and carried everything here."

"Quite a job," I said.

"A lot of paper," Morganstern said. "Bindings, glue. You know what's by the left wall?"

"No."

"My discards. Books I've worked with for years. Do you know what's over there? My favorite astronomy book. Out. I was rereading the section about quasars. Then it came to me that the book had to go. You don't notice at first. I mean my mind was on the word configuration before I saw that the quasar was called Sonyian."

170

"Yes," I said.

"Tell me what to keep," he said. "The list."

"A bit heavy on mysticism," I said.

"You think so?"

"Take for instance *Aham Brahma Asmi.*"

Morganstern sat very still. He might have been meditating. Then he opened his eyes and stared up at me.

"What else?" he said. "Pick another one."

"You might want to get rid of the account of the famous planned murders of the eighteenth century in Belgium as told to Toulan. That's an account of—"

"I know what that's an account of," Morganstern said.

"The police commissioner," I said. "The police commissioner Trasker found these old records about Madame Haldane and gave them to Toulan."

Morganstern began hunting for the book, making an avalanche of the stacks around him. He was on his knees. He looked unhappy.

"Look," I said, "could I tell you about a recurring dream I have?"

"No dreams," Morganstern whispered, pawing his books. "Not in crisis intervention.

"This is it, isn't it?" he said. He began to read. *"When Trasker brought the stranger to the house near the Bois de Boulogne station, it was late March but still cold, and snow fell regularly, as if on a schedule more exact than that of the trains. Everyone believed that it was the first time that the stranger had been there. Everyone except Giselle. They were all talking at once to prevent the stranger from hearing the scene that was at that very moment occurring in the drawing room.*

" 'You!' Madame Haldane exclaimed. 'You have cheated, lied, deceived us. Did you think that we would not find out? What else could we expect from someone like you! With a mother like yours!' "

Morganstern closed the book. "Do you want this one?" he asked.

"No," I said. "I have two copies. Couldn't we consider the dream? I have it at least twice a month."

"No dreams," Morganstern said. He coughed, shoved some papers away from his leg. "What else?"

I coughed. "The one there at the top of the stack by your left shoulder."

"That's a guide to restaurants—a guide to underground restaurants," he said.

"Under *Exotic*," I said.

Morganstern flipped through the pages. *"Giselle's,"* he read. *"Four stars. This unique restaurant specializes in fitting food to astrological signs. Heavy on spices, aromas—the tea alone is worth the trip."*

"Look," I said, "I don't think that you are well. You look drained, white, ill."

"Go on," Morganstern said. "How about this? Yes, how about this?"

"It depends upon the edition you have," I said. "I think that in that one it's on page forty-seven."

Morganstern pointed.

"That," I said. "About the Crusades."

"The Crusades?"

"Eleanor of Aquitaine has her fortune told by Sonya. It's what explains why she never went to England."

"Association," Morganstern said. "We are now going to try association."

"Association?"

"Association, association," he shouted. He struggled with his control. "All right," he said. "I say something— then you say something. Must I clarify further? Are you dense?"

"Now," I said, "I've got it."

"Cheever."

"That one."

"That one?"

"Try page one-oh-six."

"He saw her first at the supermarket. She wore a black

dress, pearls. She didn't look like anyone else. She had her children with her. His were at home. He remembered meeting her at the PTA. He remembered her. 'Giselle,' he said. She turned, frowned, yet obviously he knew her. 'Well, hello,' she said cautiously. One child pulled at her hand. 'I want Daddy,' Grace whined."

The book went to the left. All of those books went to the left.

"Is this hour being timed?" I said.

"Free," Morganstern said. "Free."

"That one," I said. "That one in chapter ten. The blue cover."

"Malamud?"

Morganstern threw two books at the wall before he reached the blue one. *"Trasker squatted in the corner,"* he read. *"He was at work when she came. He really didn't like her coming there, seeing him that way. He knew how he looked, ink all over him, dirty, unsafe. She was all right, though. It was how she was that kept Mikhail and Alekseyevich quiet. She was a lady in that thin green cotton dress. 'This is where I work,' Trasker said. 'It's dark, but I don't mind. Don't lean on anything,' he advised. 'Not the walls, not anything. Ink,' he said, 'it's everywhere.' He held out his hands, black, with a glow of carbon on them, a patina. She thought they must never be really clean. 'Let's step aside a bit,' he said. 'Our business after all. Now I've checked the deal out. It's all right.' She was small, short. He didn't know why he had wanted her. 'I felt something,' she said. 'Like a rustle, a movement against my foot.' 'Nothing,' he said, 'it's nothing, maybe paper strips moved by the fan.' He thought perhaps a rat, but no need to tell her."*

"How about poetry?" I said.

"Poetry?"

"The Penguin on the bottom of that stack," I said.

"The golden light came forth," I quoted. "The inscription for Mio Cid tightly bound. And Doña Sonya and Doña Giselle came forth."

"I never could see Pound," Morganstern said.

"All right," I said. "Oh, I see another."

"There?"

"Yes."

"My God, not Salinger too!"

Morganstern held the book as he read, his fingers with a fresh palsy making a thunderstorm of the pages.

"The children weren't as young as advertised," he read. *"The smallest boy was already eleven. It wasn't a good meeting there in the railroad station, the concrete littered with cans having a second try at fermenting, the benches warped by urine.*

" 'For chrissakes,' the girl said, 'a nursemaid, a nanny, a governess.'

" 'A fucking Peter Pan,' the youngest boy said. 'I bet they didn't check her references.'

"The woman stared at them. The job, she figured, was good for a week if she was careful. 'Call me Giselle,' she said, her voice cool, not trying to impress or be friendly.

"She was a pretty woman, and children do react better to a pretty woman.

" 'Who has a smoke?' she asked.

"The boys looked at each other. 'Yeah,' the tall one in the green sweater said and shook loose one cigarette from his pack.

"Giselle lit it herself. 'Okay,' she said. 'I don't take any crap. I don't supply any storybook fantasies, no sexual initiations. Study, pay attention.' She would, she guessed, endure the people."

Morganstern dropped the book.

"I have something else," he said. "Also, I have something else." He made a geyser of paper scraps. His forehead was moist. "This morning," he said, "carrying the books, a piece of paper dropped out. Dropped from some book. Who knows which? Wait, I have it. This piece of newsprint torn from a daily. An advertisement for a movie. I turned it over. See here? Walter Winchell's

174

column, a column by the late Walter Winchell. Part of an old column—*Who was G. with last night at the Trocadero? Who was the mysterious man with the ever-lovely G?*

"You think I didn't get that?" Morganstern went back up on his knees. "Then here, look at this thing ripped from my wife's magazine. *'This,'* Trasker says, *'is the breakfast food of champions.'*"

Morganstern collapsed back onto the floor, his arms and legs snapping against his sides like a furled umbrella.

I noticed the silver twinkle of *Eine Leerstelle* among the fallen books.

"I better leave now," I said and stood up. "Unless you'd like me to help you clean and put away. I'd certainly be willing to do that."

"What shall I do?" Morganstern said. "What shall I do about the rest of them? I want, you see, I want authenticity. Authenticity at all costs. Finish the list. You have to finish the list."

I shook my head and left the room, gently closing the door behind me. There were ten people on the street. A man carrying a cane was chasing another man, but neither of them said anything as they ran.

Twenty

All that was yesterday. I was still pleased. A decision after all is a decision. The groceries arrived from Gristede's. I had purchased many out-of-season items. I had volunteered to make Huldie's wedding feast, using the original recipes for the dinner given for the marriage of the Crown Prince of Prussia and his mistress, the mother of his only child. Tomorrow I would seek out other markets. I needed trout, a special butter, a rare wine. I certainly didn't have to consider costs.

Clothes? Should I buy a new dress for Huldie's wedding? I could wear my black lace. Perhaps liven it up with some white flowers. Would the sleeves cover my arm now painted with gentian violet, a soft, velvety shade? No, I'd buy new.

Meanwhile, the rooms were filled with the rich, fragrant odors of my purchases, odors that seemed like colors, like red and pink.

"Tricks can go just as far," Quayle said.

I thought that he might be baring his teeth. "Busy," I said and hung up.

I wiggled my fingers, hard work ahead. The arm was functioning. I went into my alcove to read. The morning newspaper told how an old woman had been arrested in Forest Hills, on a street in Forest Hills. It was the result of the employment of modern police techniques and a computer. "At first," the arresting officer said, "we didn't put two and two together. But then the printout came in.

"Three times the old lady has struck. Once with a knife, twice with a gun. She gives us this tale about jumping. The Jumper, we call her."

I cut out the article and pinned it on my bulletin board. There was no time for notes. I had to start the wedding cake by three o'clock. Huldie's cake had to be made today. The recipe required that it rest after the layers were put together. So many ingredients. I was not cutting the recipe. We could give away the leftovers. It would be a triumph. I intended no flowers for the table—just the cake in a magnificent flow of cream. Harry had promised to buy the nuts from that store on the Lower East Side. I'm baking the cake in the afternoon, I had told him. That's when I need the nuts. But I didn't count on that. I had the nuts tucked away in a bag hidden among the potatoes.

"Here they are," he said and put the bag on the counter, "less two ounces."

"Why?"

"I ate them," Harry said. "I noshed all the way over."

"You look good," I said. "Nuts become you. Nice jacket."

"Don't be nasty," Harry said. He leaned against the refrigerator. "I don't have to tell the kids," he said.

"Tell them what?"

"About Iowa. I'm not going," he said. "There were complications. Ackman's wife doesn't want to go. No plant, she said. We met with her. Tea at the Plaza. I read those tea leaves right. No, she said. No factory in Iowa. No factory anywhere."

"Yes," I said, measuring the flour. "Move away from the refrigerator," I said. "I need eggs."

"Hell," Harry said. "There's a literal quality in you, May, that I just cannot stand. You have no sense of the dream. I'm leaving."

There were twenty-three ingredients in this cake, so it would be easy to make a mistake. I would be careful. I felt good. I felt splendid. I whistled as I took the first layers of cake from the oven. My stove was no special appliance, and I could only make two layers at a time. There would be eight for this cake. I had bought new pans. The rooms now had a different smell. A blend of vanilla, lemon, rum, and sweet, rich spices.

I was concentrating. The sudden sound of the phone was like a pounding. Six times it rang. I always felt impelled to answer the phone. There were children involved, their events could not be foreseen.

"What the hell do you mean?" Quayle said. "I'm alone now. I can speak freely."

"What I meant, I said. I always try to be exact. You need a repeat? One thousand per month." I liked big round numbers.

"You're trying to up the sum—bleed the source. You shall not succeed, woman. Bear that in mind. You shall not succeed!"

"All," I said.

"Do you understand what you are doing, heartless creature? I have been fitted by my tailor. I pick up my suit this very day. At this very minute my wife is having her yellow crepe shortened. My wife is a small woman. The plane tickets have arrived. A champagne and caviar brunch has been arranged."

"Listen," I said, "could you call back later, I have to prepare a cream filling."

"This," Quayle said, "is a one-shot call. Will you accept the twenty-five thousand?"

"No," I said.

"That's it," Quayle said. "We are through. You will never hear from me again."

He hung up.

I had left the layers of cake cooling in their pans. They had to be turned onto racks, and there wasn't much time. I couldn't call him back right then.

Quayle had a fine tweed jacket woven in an ancient Druid pattern. "I'll say goodbye to you then," he said.

I must have worn my raincoat.

"Yes," I said. "Goodbye."

I folded the check.

The cake could wait. I dialed Quayle. He was right there by the phone.

"My money," I said.

"Nothing," he said, "nothing will be permitted to disrupt my trip to Sweden. I will receive that medal to glowing tributes and admiration."

"My money," I said.

"I am not stupid," Quayle said. "I have been thinking. I have realized that this is only the beginning, isn't it?"

"Yes," I said.

"After I pay you, you'll want more."

"Yes," I said.

178

"And more," Quayle said. "My God, what next? What will you want next?"

"Your wife."

"My wife?"

"Your house."

"My house?"

"Yes."

"May, do you know what this means?"

"No."

"I'll kill you!"

"What?"

"Ruin me—will you! Not this Quayle!"

He hung up.

"Wait," I yelled. I dialed his number. The phone rang, but no one answered. Four times I dialed the number. I had the operator check the phone. It was operational.

I spent an hour analyzing the characters of various famous murderers. Quayle didn't seem to fit any of those profiles. He was neither inventive, imaginative, of high intelligence, nor handicapped. He didn't even come close to anyone in Toulan's accounts. He would go off to Sweden, possibly display extreme anxiety symptoms, but he would recover. He had an intact personality. No, Quayle was not dangerous.

I had placed the last two cake pans on the wire racks to cool when the phone rang again.

"Tonight," Quayle said. This was from a phone booth, I was certain. "Tonight I will kill you, May Alto."

This was a repeat of the threat.

Now I was frightened. Character studies were of limited value after all. I paced my alcove. Quayle was going to kill me. Did that mean no payoff? No shopping bag brimming with bills? I decided that I would answer the door when he came, calmly and with dignity.

Sit down, I would say.

Why?

Let me explain, I would say.

At that point he would plunge a dagger into my heart. Or would he use a gun? Didn't I hear that Quayle was afraid of guns? Calling the police was out of the question. When I told them who was after me—and why. Sure, lady. Yeah, lady.

I remembered the most unfriendly eyes of the boys with the knife before they mugged me. I was just a random choice. No animosity intended. Just hand over the tape-recorder. A quick cut with the knife for goodbyes. I should have jumped backwards, but I didn't know how.

Would I have time to explain to Quayle? Suppose he leaped at me weapon in hand? I made it just a weapon this time. Let him choose which one. He could even do it with forty whacks.

I closed my eyes as Quayle ran screaming down the corridor babbling in tongues. *"Yafuta! Yafuta!"* He bounced from wall to wall as he made his trampoline descent to me. I would be kneeling this time, an instant convert.

I pulled my small suitcase down from the hall closet shelf. It was the suitcase that I had taken to the hospital. I packed carefully, as though for a brief outing. A change of clothes for Joanne, Richard, and Leon. I knew what else they needed, what else would make them secure, and I packed that too. On my Day-At-A-Glance calendar I neatly printed *Quayle Is Responsible* in ink, and directly beneath, I signed my name.

I shuddered at the realization of doom.

The kitchen was a mess. I was not a neat baker. Well, no need for that. Body of Woman Found in Filth, the headlines would read. I wiped up the valleys of flour, scrubbed the counters, swept the floor. The layers of cake I reluctantly wrapped in wax paper and placed in the refrigerator. I really wanted to finish that cake.

I was almost ready. All that work, all that stress had made me uncomfortable. I had to shower and fix my hair. There was also the nausea, the strange other-world taste in my mouth. Not to speak of the pain in the region of my kidneys. A yellow discharge ran freely from my arm. There was no time for the limb elevator.

The children came home from school promptly. I charted their passage across the street. They shoved and pushed at each other like strangers, but reformed as a group when they reached the curb. Their jackets were of bright colors, their choice.

I met them at the door. "Hello," I said, trying not to be cheery and thus make them suspicious. "Don't scatter. Collect any books for homework. Dinner tonight at Burger King."

"Swell," Richard said. "Can I have two shakes?"

"Shut up," Joanne said, and poked at his thigh with her tool kit. "What's the suitcase for?"

Everyone turned to look at the suitcase.

"Tonight," I said, "you go to Grace's. I'm going to call her now."

"Why?" Joanne's voice was hostile.

"I have a meeting here tonight," I said. "Big meeting—huge work assignment. I must have complete peace."

"Grace's kids stink," Leon said. "I hate Burger King."

"Go get your books," Joanne said. She was very bossy. The boys obeyed.

Joanne followed me into the kitchen. "Don't give me that stuff," she said. "We never had to go before. Who is it? Is it the poet?"

"No," I said. "Not him." That was stupid. I should have said yes.

"I don't want to go," Joanne said. "Something is up."

"Nothing is up." I was irritated. "Tomorrow after school you come home. No big deal."

"I'm not going."

"Yes, you are." I stood tall and angry in front of her.

Joanne stared right back. "We can handle trouble," she said. "Richard, Leon, and me. We're pretty strong together. We've ganged up on plenty of creeps."

"To Grace's," I said. I had to be careful not to rub my arm.

I went into the alcove to call. "Can my kids spend the night? Joanne can babysit if you want," I said to Grace.

"You need privacy?" Grace said. "You've met someone?"

That was Grace. One of the few people who remembered some of the events that I remembered, although differently. Grace had lent me a lipstick, a dress. She had sent me straight down the path to romance.

"It's trouble, Grace," I said.

"What kind? Sexual?"

"No," I said, answering the race of my heart. I couldn't explain everything. Grace didn't need to hear everything. "A client," I said. "There will be trouble."

"Real trouble?"

"He's threatening me."

"My God, call the police."

"I can't."

Now Grace and I had been children together. There had been difficult times.

"When?" she said.

"Tonight."

"I'll be over. I'll bring the others."

My children were noisy in the hall. They had acquired another suitcase, a knapsack, a brown paper bag. It was a safari, an expedition. They looked at me, waifs in a storm.

"Go to Grace's," I said. I kissed each in turn.

Alone in the apartment, I considered my health—the questions of adrenalin level, heartbeat, pulse rate, other vital signs, and the tightening at the back of my neck. I showered again to calm my spirit. Letting the warm water beat against my skin felt good. But I couldn't shower forever—suppose the phone rang?

I've changed my mind, Quayle would say.

I put on a grey wool dress, gold earrings. I carefully

brushed my hair. I didn't feel like eating dinner. Actually, I could not swallow.

If I had five minutes, certainly I would be able to explain to Quayle, make him feel less trapped, caught in a maze. He was, after all, a practical man.

I went into Joanne's room for the copy of *Eine Leerstelle*. I tore corners off pages of yesterday's newspapers for markers. I could quote from *Eine Leerstelle*. There were parts that Quayle was obviously unfamiliar with—I would read those. Pay attention, I'd say. This will help.

It wasn't helping me though. My tongue began to cleave to the dry roof of my mouth. I went to the phone. What I needed was a confessor.

I still had his number. He had given me a special private number. Did he change it every so often? I dialed the number, it rang twice, and he answered. It was after office hours.

"Morganstern," I said, "it's happened."

"Who is this?"

"May."

"Called about the list, have you," he said.

"The list?"

"My book list," Morganstern said.

"No," I said. "Not about the list. I must talk to you."

"Not the list?"

"I've been threatened, Morganstern. Hear that? He's coming for me."

Morganstern coughed. "The blackmailee?"

"Yes, him."

"I warned you. Didn't I warn you? Call the police. Your only choice, May. Call the cops."

"I can't," I said.

"Jail. You are afraid of jail—yes, I understand. But you wére warned. The victim turns. I told you that. Zap, he turns. Still, you must call the police."

"The truth isn't possible," I said. "They won't believe me."

"May, call the police. You are being threatened. We all have to face reality—this man may actually do you harm."

"He's going to kill me."

"Kill you? The man is going to kill you?"

I believed it. Suddenly, as if winds from the north had swept me clean, I believed it. I had gone too far. He was going to kill me. This Quayle who as a boy had gotten away with it all—the cheating, the money, the pregnant girl. This Quayle knew how to get away with it all. It was too late to take the money.

"Yes," I said, "the man is going to kill me."

"Who, May? Who?"

"Quayle," I said.

"What?" Morganstern was stuttering. "Did you say *Quayle?* Did I hear you say *Quayle?*"

"*Eine Leerstelle*," I said.

There was silence. Was he still there?

"Hey, Morganstern," I yelled. "What about Quayle?"

There was no reply. The phone now buzzing in my hand was alive and dead.

I went into my alcove to collect my thoughts. If I somehow missed this confrontation with Quayle, wouldn't I merely be prolonging the end of the war? He'd find me yet, on the street, in the library. No, better to face him tonight when I would be prepared. "Meet all events," my mother said. "But be careful," Aunt Giselle added.

It was already dark out. I ran around the apartment pulling all the shades. Did he know which windows were mine? Never mind. Better safe than sorry, as my mother used to say. The door was bolted.

The phone rang. I thought it might be Morganstern. It was Quayle.

"I'm on the way, woman," he said. "This is how it will end, you made it end this way, you predicted it."

"I didn't," I said. "You're wrong. In *Eine Leerstelle*, man may be a brute, but he is always overcome by civilizing forces."

184

"The hell with *Eine Leerstelle*," Quayle said.

"It's a question of understanding," I said, paraphrasing my mother. "We all have more than one chance."

"Not you," Quayle said without hesitation, and hung up.

I went back into my alcove and pulled down my Quayle folder. Was there a clue? A key to the man? I read through papers, clippings. "After I pay you, you'll want more," he had said. He was right.

Nominations of Nobel Prize candidates, I read, *must reach the Nobel Committees before February 1st of the year in which the award is to be made. Nominations should be in writing and accompanied by published material in support.*

That too was in the folder.

Even now while Quayle was advancing towards me, the Committees were at work on next year's selections.

Quayle was coming. I had to prepare. "Come on then, come on you Quayle," I said. I went into the kitchen for my cast iron frying pan. It was the nearest thing to a weapon that I could imagine. I certainly wasn't going to stab him. I stood in the living room and practiced a few swings. I had to be careful of my sore arm.

"It's us," Grace called before pushing the doorbell.

"Just a moment," I said, putting down the frying pan before I hurried to the door.

There they were—the three of them. Grace and Huldie and Rosemary.

"Are you alone?" Huldie asked.

"Yes," I said.

"Let us in," Grace said. "We can't stand in the hall."

I stepped back. "Yes, yes," I said. "I'm sorry to bring you out this way."

"What are friends for?" Grace said.

They came into the living room. I took their coats and put them in the hall closet. Rosemary hung onto her shopping bag. "My arsenal," she said. "I took them from the kids."

185

Everyone smoothed their dresses. They all looked nice. It was an evening out. Everyone wore nylons and heels. Grace wore her mother's locket.

"Do you think that the lights should be on?" Huldie said.

"This far above the street?" Rosemary said. "Don't be silly."

"Shall I make some coffee?" I said.

"Brandy," Rosemary said. Huldie nodded.

"Bourbon and soda," Grace said.

I went for the drinks. The banging of the ice cube tray was unnerving, but I managed. I put all the glasses on a white plastic tray and carried them back to the living room.

Grace was at the window. She had raised one shade. "Lots of bums in the park," she said.

"There always are," I said.

"There goes a man running. He's after someone—an old man, probably an experienced vandal. I think he caught him by the bushes—seems to be going at him with a club."

"You're making me nervous," Huldie said. "Sit down!"

"Just one question, May," Grace said as she sat down. "It's political, isn't it?"

"Yes," I said. "Political."

"I knew that," Grace said and exchanged glances with the others. "I've suspected for a long time that you were still involved. May is still carrying on, I said. I suspected."

"I was a lookout once," Huldie said, "back then. There was some business going on with those men from Canada. I was supposed to whistle if anyone came."

"And nothing happened. Right?" Rosemary said.

"No," Huldie said. "They came."

"Well," Grace said, "just let them try. That's all I say, just let them try."

"I made your cake today," I told Huldie. "I haven't frosted it yet, but it's baked."

186

I thought that Huldie's face flushed, but the lamps were on low, and I couldn't be certain. "That's great," she said.

We sat in silence. We were old friends and needn't speak all the time. Huldie suddenly leaned forward, her hearing increased by cunning, by remembering old experiences. "I think," she whispered, "that someone's in the hall. I hear sounds."

Rosemary opened her shopping bag. We were very quiet. It was the cellar again. She handed around the weapons. There were two short plastic baseball bats, red and yellow, and a boomerang. The weapons were nestled across silken laps, and we waited.

The doorbell sounded. I stood up, feeling more secure. "Yes," I called.

"It's me," Harry said. "Open the door."

There were quizzical looks, but I knew the voice.

I opened the door. He was alone. He had a large paper bag. "Why is it so dark in here?" he said. "Hello, girls."

He would have kissed my cheek, but I stepped back. He handed me the bag. "At least I bought enough ice cream," he said. "What have I interrupted?"

"You don't know, do you?" Grace said with scorn. "You just don't know, Harry."

"That is possibly true," he said. "What?"

"May has been threatened."

"Another mugging? You'll have to move."

"Not a mugging," I said. "A client."

"Did you call the police?"

"I can't," I said. "That's not possible."

Harry understood about such matters. He put his hands in his pockets and went into the living room. "Where are the kids?"

"Safe," I said. "They're at Grace's."

We sat there, waiting through the evening hours. Later I made some coffee and served dishes of Harry's ice cream. Someone suggested the radio, and we listened to dance music. But we remained alert and ready.

"Why don't we all go out," Rosemary said. "I feel a need to be out."

Grace looked uneasy. "We can't all fit into Hers," she said. "Hers is getting too old to carry a heavy load."

"No," Huldie said, 'we should stay here. They always advised being indoors."

Twice, I found an excuse to go into the kitchen where the light was brighter. I had a notebook there. A lot of things were happening. I described the weapons, the quality of Grace's voice, the time when Huldie was a lookout. I described the loss of great sums of money due to a disaster. I put the pad back on top of the refrigerator. I was still in the kitchen when the pounding began rather suddenly. It was accompanied by loud roars.

"I'll get the door," I said.

"Let's all go," Grace said.

"No!"

"Call out if you need help," Harry said.

I was at the door, feeling the varnish-smoothed wood vibrate from the acrobatics of fists. The shrieks, the cries, the growls turning into an inspiration of music. I thought of the second act of *Die Götterdämmerung* in the hall of Gilich when Alberic tries to persuade Hagen to win back the ring. Or even the last movement of Honegger's *Concertino*. What color! What sonority! What tone!

"Are you there?" Quayle hissed.

I didn't answer. I leaned forward, palms against the door, an exercise in balance. Quayle was out there with his muzzle-loading revolvers, knives, lengths of cord, gas chambers, döppelgangers, poison-bearing pins. Where was the door from? *House in the Hills, House of Joy, House of Mirth, House of Souls, House of the Dead, House of the Seven Gables*—all those doors were mine!

I turned around to see my friends sitting on the couch, smiling encouragingly, and waving their plastic bats.

Still at the door, I considered what was on my side, the level of my strength—jumping backwards, the good arm—also taking into account the weaknesses and pre-dilections of the reader.

So I faced up to the truth—I could not be defeated. I knew what the reader wanted. I took unto me full responsibility for what was mine. There was victory in me, a great swelling of triumph.

Open the door to Quayle?

Hell, why the fuck not!

Shirley Eskapa
The Secret Keeper

'Shirley Eskapa's *The Secret Keeper* is a psychological study of an eternal triangle, the difference being that the child stands in as the eyes for the mother. Set in the claustrophobic atmosphere of Geneva's expatriate society, it is gradually revealed that the absent mother is working through the son she appeared to have left behind in order to wreak her vengeance on the mistress. Ms Eskapa is excellent at evoking the hothouse atmosphere of international finance and in seeing into the mind of a confused adolescent' OVER 21

'Shirley Eskapa's handling of the boy's point of view through his secret diaries is convincing and perceptive – she tells a gripping story with deftness and considerable insight' MIRANDA SEYMOUR, THE TIMES

'I enjoyed it so much – a beautifully sharp description of Geneva life' H. R. F. KEATING

'Sophisticated and sharp-eyed' COMPANY

'*The Secret Keeper* is a masterful study of suspense, emotion and the highly disturbing implications of a torrid love affair plus the disasters of parenthood. The story is as taut as a violin string, controlled, subtle and intense, dealing with the clever manipulations of loving and supposedly caring mothers' SUNDAY EXPRESS

'This is a sparse, economical book written in a style taut and clipped, admirably suited to its hidden tensions. To create character through a journal is tricky enough but to base the whole plot on the diary of a thirteen-year-old is little short of foolhardy. That Shirley Eskapa just about avoids the pitfalls of such a device is proof enough of her considerable self-assurance' LITERARY REVIEW

Jane Beeson
Apple of an Eye

'A wonderfully powerful book' FAY WELDON

Jane Beeson's first novel is set on the Devon Moors and tells the story of Tamsin Band, an adolescent girl who lives on a remote farm with her drunken father, younger brother and her strict, church-going aunt. Ten years earlier her mother ran away from the claustrophobic atmosphere; now Tamsin learns she is back – not with her family – but living in a nearby farm with a boyfriend half her age. The day Tamsin crosses the moors for a secret reunion with her mother is the beginning of a time in her life which will end in tragedy and death.

Writing about tragedy and passion in rural England, Jane Beeson's work has been compared to that of Thomas Hardy and H. E. Bates.

'Jane Beeson is an excellent writer – I read *Apple of an Eye* through in one sitting because I was engrossed in the story. She has a very sure ear and touch for terror – there is a great deal of power in her writing' ERIN PIZZEY

A Winter Harvest

Jane Beeson's second novel is also set on the Devon moors and is based on her own scripts for a dramatic 5-part television serial on BBC2 starring Cheryl Campbell from the *Testament of Youth* serial and *Chariots of Fire*.

It tells the story of Caroline Ashurst whose husband Patrick goes into hospital leaving her to run their remote moorland farm, a role for which she is ill-equipped.

Susanna Moore
My Old Sweetheart

Hawaii in the 1950s is the idyllic setting for Susanna Moore's very special, highly praised first novel. But against the tropical splendour is played a family drama of frightening intensity.

Lily is a little girl growing up in Paradise: her father is a distinguished and respected doctor, her mother is a stunning beauty. But why is her mother taking drugs, indulging in increasingly erratic behaviour and apparently heading for an early death – as though on purpose? Why does her charismatic father behave so coldly and often cruelly to his wife, supplying her with drugs, spurning her for the charms of a simple Hawaiian girl?

Lily observes this horrific conflict from the bewildered innocence of childhood. As tragedy takes its inevitable course and as Lily grows to womanhood, we are mesmerised by this powerful tale of hell in paradise, a story strangely resolved in Lily's final quest through the madness of Pol Pot's Cambodia in search of her father.

My Old Sweetheart is filled with the sights, sounds and smells of Hawaii before Pan Am and the Hilton – a Hawaii that Jean Rhys would have recognized – a luxurious Hawaii personified by Lily's mother Anna who arrives at a ball in a cape made of four thosand gardenias . . . The sensual power of this remarkable first novel was not lost on Susanna Moore's critics.

'A marvellous, intense first novel by an American, but often remarkably English in feeling. Susanna Moore's touch is sure and her eye is piercing. Her book is full of those vivid, haunting scenes which reveal a whole emotional history. Sad, unsentimental and magical'
GRAHAM SWIFT, SUNDAY TIMES

'Brilliant . . . beautifully written. An enchanting first novel'
STEPHEN SPENDER

'A gem of a book' COMPANY

'The lush atmosphere of Hawaii hangs over the reader's armchair . . . Susanna Moore is a gifted and compelling novelist, already in possession of her own unique voice'
ANNE TYLER, NEW YORK TIMES BOOK REVIEW

'Extraordinarily moving . . . I've read a lot, but I can't recall another novel like this about mothers and daughters'
SUSAN LYNDON, VILLAGE VOICE